The Big Goodbye

Books by Michael Lister

Power in the Blood
Blood of the Lamb
Flesh and Blood
North Florida Noir
Double Exposure
Thunder Beach
Florida Heat Wave
The Body and the Blood
The Big Goodbye
The Meaning of Life in Movies
Finding the Way Again
Blood Sacrifice
Burnt Offerings
Separation Anxiety

The Big Goodbye
Michael Lister

a novel

PULPWOOD PRESS

Panama City, FL

Inquiries should be addressed to:
Pulpwood Press
P.O. Box 35038
Panama City, FL 32412

Lister, Michael.
The Big Goodbye / Michael
Lister.
-----1st ed.
p.   cm.
ISBN: 978-1888146-78-3 (hardback)
ISBN: 978-1-888146-79-0 (trade paperback)
ISBN: 978-1-888146-80-6 (ebook)

Library of Congress Control Number:

Book Design by Adam Ake

Printed in the United States

1 3 5 7 9 10 8 6 4 2

First Edition

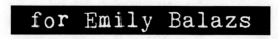

for Emily Balazs

Chapter 1

I had not yet recovered from shooting Stanley Somerset when I saw her.

Part of me hoped I'd never see her again. Part of me was constantly looking for her, scanning every crowd, straining to see around every corner, peering into every slowly passing car.

The funny thing was, I only saw her on that rarest of occasions when I wasn't looking for her—like when I was in the middle of a case, having just shot a man.

Ray and I had been hired by a voice on the phone and a check in the mail to locate a sixteen-year-old runaway from Nag's Head, North Carolina.

It hadn't been difficult. The man she had run away with—her forty-eight-year-old step-dad—who had a room in the Dixie Sherman Hotel downtown wasn't capable of keeping a low profile.

"It just don't add up. You gonna run to Panama City, you stay at the beach, right?" July, our part-time secretary, said from the backseat of Ray's big Packard. "Why bring her to the Dixie?"

Like Ray, the car was squarish and conservative, a late-model black four-door sedan that made him feel like a cop.

We were parked on Fifth Street beneath a warm October sun, the planted palms lining the sidewalks flapping in the wind, unable to provide any shade.

"Dixie Sherman's nice," Ray said. "Besides, they got beaches where they ran away from."

Ray Parker, former Pinkerton agent, had seen the world—or so it seemed to me and July. The two of us had barely left Bay County. He was nearly twice as old as we were—wise, too. We never doubted a word he spoke—which was easier than you might imagine. Buttoned up Ray rarely spoke. He was obviously pleased by the possibility of pinching the kind of creep who'd run off with a little girl. We all were.

"Jimmy, you know what I mean, don't you?" July asked me. "Why bring her here at all?"

She wore her hair in a short feather cut, pincurls around her ears and on top of her head. She did this, she had confided in me one time, to de-emphasize the roundness of her full face, which was just silly. She had a cute face and a long, thin neck. Girls can be so silly sometimes.

"For what we *don't* have," I said. "The lady paying our bills."

"The wife," July said.

"The *mother*," Ray said.

Sitting at the corner of Jenks and Fifth Street, the Dixie Sherman, the only high-rise around, was built in 1925 by W. C. Sherman, and had one hundred and one rooms, each with a bathroom, a telephone, and elegant furniture—all starting at just three bucks.

When it opened in 1926 many locals referred to it as the "white elephant" downtown and called it "too much hotel" for the area, and maybe it was—back then, but here in the fall of 1943 its rooms were always full and its dance floors were the place to be on a Saturday night.

The couple in question pulled up in a new blue torpedo sport coupe Pontiac, parked, and walked into the lobby.

Thunk.

Thunk.

Thunk.

Three slamming car doors later we were following behind them.

July didn't usually tag along, but Ray thought she might cozy up to the little sixteen-year-old dumb Dora while we put the cure on her daddy. Ray had saved July's life on a case he worked before I joined the agency, and had been saving her ever since. She wasn't much of a secretary, but then there wasn't much we needed a secretary for. She was stuck on Ray, looked at him in that dreamy, wide-eyed I-owe-you-my-life way that's worth shelling out the dough of a part-time salary for.

Though Ray hadn't been a cop for a long time, he still stood out like one, so while July and I hopped the elevator with Stanley and his stepdaughter, Ray took the stairs.

As the elevator ascended, I pretended to be keen on July, which wasn't hard to do. What was hard was groping her with one arm, but she was swell about it, and as I kissed her neck, she coyly fought off my advances. When the doors opened on their floor and they stepped out into the empty corridor, Stanley looked back and said, "Come on, mister, at least wait'll you get to your room."

"Don't get your pulleys all twisted up, you old fuddy-duddy," July said, pretending to try to get at him as I held her back. "Ain't like this is Fifth Avenue or somethin'."

I nodded toward my missing arm. "Just got back from the war and I'm a little overheated. Didn't mean no harm. Sorry your little girl had to see it."

"That's okay, soldier," he said. "We all appreciate what you boys—"

"That ain't *his* little girl," July said. "Look at her. She's a doll for creeps like 'em young."

Just as he was supposed to, the man stepped toward us, preparing to protect the dignity of his daughter-bride.

I snapped out a hard left jab—well, as hard as I could with my left—and the punch caught him square on his left cheek.

He staggered back a bit, but didn't go down.

So I hit him again. This time, a left hook that connected with his right cheek and buckled his knees. He went down, the closing elevator doors bumping into his prostrate body as he did.

Before I could grab him, little Lisa was on top of him, making sure he was okay between turning and yelling obscenities at me.

"We're here to take you home, Lisa," I said.

And that was my mistake.

They both perked up when they heard me use her name.

"Your mom hired us to find you and bring you home," I continued, unaware a guy as sick as Stanley would be paranoid enough to suspect something like this.

"I won't go," she said.

"Oh yes you will," I said, reaching down and grabbing her. "And your daddy's going to jail."

When I pulled her off him, Stanley came up with a gun.

That's me, Jimmy Riley, boy genius.

"Stupid son of a bitch," I said.

"On the contrary," Stanley said. "I was ready for—"

"He's talking about himself," Ray said as he walked up behind Stanley with a gun of his own. "He should've known you'd be packin' a rod. Put down the heater, Stanley," Ray said. "I'm a very good shot."

"Okay," Stanley said, dropping his head and lowering his gun.

Suddenly, he grabbed Lisa, spinning her around for a shield and sticking the gun to the side of her head.

"Put *your* gun down."

Behind Stanley I withdrew mine as Ray placed his on the ground.

"Just relax," Ray was saying.

Stanley spun around to face us, placing Lisa between us.

"Get around there with him," he yelled. "Drop your gun."

We did and I did, my little revolver clanking against Ray's as it hit the floor.

"We don't want to live if we can't be together," Stanley said.

"I'm not going back," Lisa said. "I'd rather die." She then cut her wide and wild eyes up toward Stanley. "I'm tired of running. Tired of her chasing us. Shoot me, baby. Let's die together. Today. Right here. Right now. She'll just keep sending 'em. She don't understand. Nobody does."

Stanley nodded.

"Kick the guns away from you," he said.

We did.

"Kneel down."

We did.

"Stanley," July said, "she's clearly an unstable and melodramatic little girl. What's your excuse?"

"She can't understand," Lisa said to him. "She's never been in love."

As they talked, I felt back to the .22 in my ankle holster with my left hand. My movements were awkward and clumsy. I hadn't gotten used to using my left yet.

Coughing to cover the sound, I pulled it free.

"Honey, this ain't love," July said. "It only feels like it. You're the one who's never been loved."

"Why you fuckin' floozy," Lisa said, then turning back to Stanley, "Bump her off, too, Daddy. Do it for me. Whatta you say?"

Stanley thought about it for a minute, then nodded.

At that, Lisa lit up. Bending over toward July and sticking her face out like a child much younger than she was, she said, "Guess who's gonna take a powder with us, huh? Huh?"

When Stanley let go of Lisa and raised his gun toward July, Ray lunged toward him as I brought up the small revolver and fired it.

The bullet hit his right leg just before he squeezed off a round. He flinched and missed July, the bullet lodging in the elevator wall behind us. Before he could fire again, Ray had tackled him to the ground and taken away his weapon.

Lisa dove for our guns, still on the floor about five feet away, but July kicked them out of reach. She then jumped up and began flailing at July, who easily blocked most of the kicks and hits, and, quickly growing weary, slugged her in the stomach. She doubled over, trying to take in air, but nothing happened. When she finally could take a breath, she began to cry.

A couple of hours later, after Lisa had been picked up by a rotund police matron, and Stanley had been taken into custody and to Lisenby Hospital to have the bullet removed, and my old partner had taken our statements and let us go, the three of us were riding back down in the elevator.

"She was right," July said almost to herself.

When Ray didn't say anything, I said, "About what?"

"I never *have* been in love."

"Neither has she," I said.

"Have you?" she asked me.

I nodded, images of Lauren flashing in my mind like buoys bobbing in the bay on a stormy night, not daring to speak for fear of what might come out.

"Was it anything like that?"

I remembered how gladly I would have died for Lauren when we were together, how badly I had wanted to die when she left me. I recalled the passion and obsession that had so often bordered on madness, and the way in which nothing else in the world seemed to matter—no, that's not exactly it, the way there didn't seem to be anything else in the world when we were together.

I shook my head. "No. Nothing like that."

And then the elevator doors opened and Lauren was standing there with a dandy I didn't recognize—the poor grotty sap she had her hooks in now.

The timing couldn't have been worse. I still had the jeebies from shooting Stanley, still raw from the memories July's questions had resurrected.

Time seemed to stop as I projected onto him all her lies and betrayal. Instantly, standing there all togged to the bricks and high-hating, he embodied all I hated about her faithlessness and my weakness.

Before I realized what I was doing, I had knocked him down, pinned him to the ground with my body, and was punching him repeatedly in the face with the bottom of my left fist.

Friend and father figure that he was, Ray pulled me off him, and when I tried to get through him to continue my assault, he committed a little assault of his own—on me.

Chapter 2

"I hope he'll be all right," Ruth Ann said.

"She'll do far worse to him," I said.

We were sitting at the bar in Nick's.

"Gee, mister, who gave you such a high opinion of women?" she asked, smiling before she took the next sip of her drink.

The playful question was rhetorical, so I didn't answer. She knew damn well.

Nick's was a small, dark bar that served hard, cheap liquor and lots of it. It had a Wurlitzer jukebox with fluorescent lighting, a small dance floor, and a couple of pool tables in a room in the back.

Ruth Ann Johnson, a Salvation Army nurse, and I often met here for drinks and conversation late at night when the place was filled with our kind of people. I was nursing a tall-neck bottle of Schlitz, staring into the large mirror on the wall behind the bar. She sat beside me sipping on a martini. In the mirror, I could see a few couples dancing in front of the jukebox, the colorful lights of its pipes and grille panels flashing on their faces. Beyond them in the back room, a handful of men in uniform from Tyndall Field and the naval section base were drinking and shooting pool like they meant it.

"I'm worried about you," she said.

"Because I hit a guy?"

"Hit? You pummeled him, soldier, and you know it."

I didn't say anything. I had asked her not to call me that, but the more I asked, the more she said it. She knew better, but it was an assumption nearly every stranger made. I hadn't been wounded in combat. I never got to serve. I got tangled up with the serious-intentioned end of a shotgun while I was still with the Panama City Police Department and any hopes I had of serving went the way of my right arm.

Unlike me, Ruth Ann had served in the war, helping wounded soldiers in the South Pacific before getting wounded herself. I think it was our wounds that made us such good drinking buddies, though we never really talked about my missing arm or her missing leg. I found mine a source of embarrassment, but I wasn't sure why she avoided the subject of her heroism.

"You think he'll press charges?" she asked.

I shrugged. "Probably not if it means explaining to his wife why he was at a swanky hotel with another doll."

"How you know he's married?"

"It's my business," I said with a smile.

I glanced at the bullet hole in the mirror behind the bar, the web-like veins spreading out from it, and recalled a recent case of marital unhappiness involving Angel Adams and her hood husband, Mickey.

"I thought trouble was your business?"

I laughed.

Though I'd never seen her get all dolled up, not even once, Ruth Ann was still the kind of girl guys called doll. She had thick blonde hair worn above her shoulders and flipped out on the ends and big blue eyes that looked interested even when they weren't. She was small and looked like somebody's cute kid sister.

"Hey doll face."

I turned to see a sailor leaning against the bar on the other side of Ruth Ann.

"What'll you have?"

"Some more quiet conversation with my friend here," she said, jerking her head back toward me, her blonde hair swishing about as she did.

"You with lefty?" he asked, leaning around her to glare at my missing right.

Before she could answer, I spoke up.

"Tell you what," I said. "I was right-handed before it got blown off, but I'll arm wrestle you for her."

"Sure, soldier, I'll take your girl," he said.

I turned around and took a few steps so I could put my left arm on the bar and move away from our drinks some. He strutted around, placed his hat on the stool next to him and his elbow on the bar.

"Don't go nowhere doll," he said to Ruth Ann. "This'll only take a second."

The moment he finished speaking, as he was still looking at her, I reached up and grabbed the back of his head and slammed his face down into the bar. His nose and forehead smacked the marble bar top but good and it knocked him out cold. He fell to the floor face up and didn't move.

I moved back down beside Ruth Ann and took a long pull on my bottle of Schlitz, eyeing the other sailors in the mirror. I didn't think this guy was with them, and I must've been right because they continued their game without more than a passing interest in their fallen comrade.

"You not worried about being so . . . What's the word I'm looking for? . . . *eager* . . . to make with the mauling?"

"I didn't maul him," I said.

"I was talking about the guy earlier today," she said. "Jeez, you're dropping guys all over town."

I started to say something, but she cut me off. "You should talk to someone."

"I do."

"A professional."

"She is."

She turned and looked at me, her big blue eyes wide. "Really?"

"That so surprising?"

"Jimmy Riley talking to a shrink?" she said. "Well, heck yeah."

"The force sent me to her when I got shot. When I left the force I just kept going."

"Just keep the surprises coming, soldier, I don't mind," she said. "But have you considered maybe it ain't workin' so good?"

"I don't know," I said. "I didn't *kill* either of 'em."

Chapter 3

"Lauren Lewis is here to see you," July said.

My quickening pulse began to pound inside my constricting throat.

I had just returned from the small library around the block with a bag of books when July had eased into my office and closed the door behind her. She waited in front of my desk, as she always did, while I finished the sentence I was reading, and when I looked up, I caught her casting an eyeball over the novels and philosophy and psychology texts with only a mild interest.

"Really?"

Suddenly, the hairline at the top of my forehead was moist, my mouth dry.

"She asked for you, but I could take her in to see Ray."

"Show her in," I said.

"But—"

"Show her in."

Dropping the book on the scarred wooden desk with the others, I jumped up and looked out my second-story window, across downtown Panama City. The traffic on Harrison was light, the sidewalks mostly empty. The unseen morning sun behind me cast a warm glow on the sleepy streets, but I found no peace or strength in any of it, so I sat back down.

July didn't usher Lauren in so much as stand aside and allow her to enter, and I couldn't help but think that the way she stood, leaning against my door and arching her back to accentuate her nearly flawless figure, was the female equivalent of a man flexing for another man.

When Lauren had walked in, she glanced around, noting—I could tell because I knew how she thought—that in the year that had passed, the old walls had remained bare.

Unlike the first time July had shown Lauren into my office, she didn't take her coat, offer her coffee, or close the door.

I resisted the urge to stand, and I forced myself to look right into her dark eyes as if for the first time.

Swallowing hard to ensure my voice wouldn't break, I attempted a casual, "Lauren."

"Are you following me?" she asked.

For a moment I couldn't speak, guilt gripping my vocal cords.

"What?" I asked, my voice filled with a surprise as brittle as my attempt at casualness had been.

I tried to laugh it off as inane or absurd, but images of a desperate man hiding in the shadows undermined my attempt. Nearly a year had passed, and I didn't recognize that man any longer, but I still hated his helplessness, loathed his lack of self-control. His existence had been a brief and solitary one. Lauren never knew of it. As far as I knew, only my counselor did.

"I remember one time you said if you ever wanted to follow me I'd never know it, but . . ."

"I'm not following you," I said as if I never had, my voice filled with the wounded pride of an innocent man.

She collapsed back in her chair and the familiar scent of Paris perfume drifted across my desk.

Beneath her dark brown hair, combed smooth across the top and hanging in soft curls above her shoulders, her flawless skin seemed nearly too perfect, the almond eyes beneath the razor sharp eyebrows nearly too dark, too deep, too . . . Nearly, but not too.

From my inside right coat pocket, the only inside pocket I was able to use, I pulled out a pack of Pall Malls, shook out two, put them in my mouth, and returned the pack to my pocket. I then fished in my left outside pocket for a lighter. This all took a while and she waited patiently. Once I had them both lit, I took one out and held it out to her. She stood and accepted my offering, placing what had just been in my mouth between her Revlon-red lips. She then took a long drag from the cigarette, held it a moment, and lifted her head to blow it out slowly.

"How are you doing with . . . ," she asked, nodding toward where my right arm should be.

I had been injured the day she left me—as a result of her leaving me, but she didn't know that—and we hadn't really spoken since then. I was still on the force, but moonlighting for Ray when I took her case. I was wounded in the line of duty, called a hero, awarded citations, but if I hadn't been working with Ray, if I hadn't taken her case, if I had never met her, it would have never happened.

"I manage," I said. "Ladies like a wounded war hero. They think some Jap bastard blew it off. I straighten them out . . . eventually."

I wondered if she could tell I was lying. I hadn't been with a woman since her, couldn't if I wanted to. Could she tell? Was she still able to see through me?

"I was so sorry to hear it had happened," she said. "But I was very proud of you, too. You were so brave. That woman and her child owe you their lives."

The truth was, I hadn't been brave so much as numb. If I hadn't been, I would have waited for backup. I didn't care if I died. In fact,

I wanted to. I wasn't brave. I was suicidal—and it cost me far more than my right arm, but she'd never know that.

When she sat down again, we were quiet a moment longer.

Her silhouette-style black dress emphasized her trim waist and narrow hips and grew broad above her breasts. The war had made stockings mostly a thing of the past, but her dress showed plenty of pale leg beneath black silk stockings, the backs of which had seams running down them. The rest of the girls had to go bare-legged and draw seams down the back of their legs with black eyeliner to give the illusion of stockings, but not Mrs. Harry Lewis. She wore them to help conceal the burn scars on her legs, but her exemption from even the smallest wartime sacrifice made me angry.

Her two-tone, thick high heels brought together the black of her dress, its white collar and highlights, and the white of her gauntlet gloves and clutch bag.

"Someone's following me," she said, her voice ragged and weary. "I thought it might be you."

"It's not—"

"Of course it's not," she said. "I don't know what I was thinking."

"—so you can mark my name off the list," I continued, "and move on to whoever came after me . . . or before—depending on how you're working your way through us."

Only the slightest twinge of pain showed on the fine features of her delicate but tense face. There was nothing I could say that would shock her. She had long since grown to expect my cruelty.

Resolutely, she stood. "Sorry to . . . I mean . . . I shouldn't've come here."

"Someone's tailing you?"

She paused to consider me, her eyes searching mine.

"Yeah," she said, slowly drifting back into her seat, "I think so."

"How long's it been going on?"

"A while," she said. "I don't know—a month at least. At first I thought it was my imagination. Then, for a while, I just dropped out of sight so he couldn't follow me. But now . . . now I can't and it's happening again."

"Obviously you haven't gotten a good look at him or you wouldn't've thought it was me," I said. "What—"

"I haven't seen him at all."

"What's he done?"

"Whatta you mean?"

"To let you know he's there," I said. "He hasn't done anything? Not to your car, your cat, your—"

"You know I don't have a cat," she said.

"I don't know what you have now," I said. "Or who. I assume you still have a husband."

"Yes," she said, gathering her purse again.

"So he hasn't done anything to you or your property?" I asked.

We aren't each other's property, I suddenly remembered her saying near the end. *No one ever owns another person. No one ever can.*

I hadn't remembered that until now. What else had I forgotten? What other shards of memory were buried so deep they could be felt but not recalled and would come unbidden, triggered by a word, a smell, a taste?

"No," she said.

I thought about that.

She looked around some more—perhaps searching for clues to my condition or any evidence that she had ever been a part of my life—and while she did, I stole glances at her. She still wore her long dark hair down over the right side of her face to conceal the burns, very little makeup, and too many clothes.

Her eyes drifted across the various stacks of books scattered around the floor, over the dusty boxing gloves to the stack of files atop the old metal filing cabinet, past the framed pictures on the floor leaning against the wall, beyond the chess board still awaiting my next move as it was the last time she was here, and came to rest on the records full of sad songs stacked on my Motorola Spinet.

What does all this tell you about the condition you left me in? What are you thinking? Feeling? Do you feel anything for me? Did you ever?

"Creeps usually do something to let you know they're there," I said. "It's their idea of a swell time. If this guy hasn't done anything . . ."

"What?"

"I don't know."

We fell silent again and I could hear July talking on her phone out in the hallway. From her serious tone and cryptic conversation I knew it was Ray.

Gracefully, Lauren crossed her long, shapely legs and straightened out her skirt. Her movements were as smooth and elegant as the silk stockings gripping her gams. As usual, they were dark, but you could still make out the burns down her right leg if you knew where to look.

Her eyes grew wide when she saw the bullet hole in the wall above my filing cabinet. "Is that a—"

"Yeah," I said. "Are you sure someone's following you?"

She shrugged. "It's more a feeling than anything else, but yeah, I'm sure."

"It's probably either an ex-lover, your husband, or a PI hired by one of them. Or both," I said. "So—"

"My only ex-lover is a PI."

I may have been her only ex-lover who was a private detective. I was not her only ex-lover. She'd tried to make it sound like the latter instead of the former.

"—you're probably not in any danger, but I'll find out who's doing it and—"

"No," she said. "I didn't come here to hire you. I just wanted to—"

She stopped abruptly as the phone on my desk began to ring.

"Sorry," I said as I snatched up the receiver.

"Don't agree to take her case or do anything for her before you talk to me," Ray whispered.

"What?"

"I'll explain when she leaves. I have relevant information."

When I hung up she said, "I'll let you go. I know you're busy."

Though the stack of books on my desk belied my busyness, I didn't contradict her.

"Okay," I said, "but don't worry about whoever's following you, I'll take care of him."

"No," she said, standing to leave. "I'm not going to hire someone to follow me because I think someone's following me. I just—"

"You're not hiring me," I said, my voice angry and hurt.

"You're right I'm not," she said, walking over to the door, "so don't follow me."

"Don't worry after me, sister, I won't be there," I said, as if I really wouldn't.

After Lauren left, I sat there for a moment, stunned, and thought back to the first time she had come into my office and disarmed me with her disconcerting honesty, unconventional beauty, and her complete lack of pretense and illusion.

My desire for her had been instant and incomprehensible.

"Of the infidelity cases you investigate, how many of the people turn out to be cheating?" she had asked.

"Nearly all."

"Really?"

"Most people don't come to us the first time they have suspicions."

"So what percentage?"

I shrugged.

"How many? I want to know."

"It's hard to say."

"How long have you been doing this?"

"A few years," I said.

It was evening. I had been moonlighting with Ray for a while, but not a few years. I was sick of swimming in the cesspool of city politics and corruption and was getting ready to leave the force. My plan had been to start working for Ray full-time when I came back from the war.

"So, of the cases you've worked, how many were guilty of cheating?"

"All of them," I said.

Her eyes widened. She then exhaled heavily and fell back into her chair, the expression on her face a curious one, as if I had just shared a strange good news.

"So the fact that I'm here almost guarantees that my husband is cheating."

"Do you love your husband?"

"Very much."

"If he is cheating, are you going to leave him?"

She shook her head.

"Then don't do this."

"I've got to," she said.

"Why? Why do you want to know?"

"I love my husband, Mr. Riley."

"So don't—"

"Like a father," she said. "I'm not *in* love with him—not like a wife. I care about him a great deal. I owe him . . . well, everything. But if I knew he had someone . . ."

She trailed off, but seemed to need to say more, so I waited.

"It would be a great comfort to me."

Chapter 4

One of the advantages of tailing someone you know intimately is you can often anticipate where she's going and get there before she does. When Lauren turned onto Beck in the direction of St. Andrews, I knew she was headed to Mattie's Tavern to meet her husband for lunch. When she pulled into the parking lot, I was waiting for her.

Located at the corner of 12th Street and Beck Avenue in St. Andrews, Mattie's Tavern was famous for its fried chicken, steaks, seafood, and hush puppies, but it wasn't the food the Lewises came for as much as all the potential voters in such close proximity.

As she made her way through the parking lot, I ducked behind a big brown Pontiac Streamline Station Wagon. When she went inside, I waited a few moments, then followed, coming up behind her in time to see the hostess ushering her past those waiting in line and escorting her to a table near the window where her husband, Harry, was already eating a salad.

Backing behind the bar, I became aware of a fluttering sensation in my chest. It took me a moment to realize it was something like happiness—a feeling I had grown unaccustomed to. I was happy just to be back in the shadows of her life again, and as much as I hated myself for that, I hated her even more.

The sound of Peggy Lee singing "The Way You Look Tonight" was coming from a juke box next to an empty dance floor.

Since Harry Lewis had announced his bid to be mayor, he and Lauren had taken every opportunity to be seen together in public. Side by side they smiled, shook hands, and spoke briefly but intimately to every one of their thousands of best friends.

With an unsettling sense of déjà vu, I recalled watching Harry before, the extravagance of his banker's lifestyle, the leisure of his banker's schedule, and the way his groveling underlings catered to his every whim—including his mistress, Martha, a bookkeeper twice as old and half as attractive Lauren.

Martha provided Lauren and me with the justification we needed to nurture our budding attraction—which we did with the wounded intensity of the wronged and the righteous indignation of the innocent, without the slightest sense of irony or hypocrisy.

With a bittersweet smile, I remembered how I had been so happy to discover her that I sent Martha flowers the day after I first caught she and Harry together.

What began as revenge became a profound love and an intoxicating passion. Soon, Harry wasn't part of our equation any longer, and eventually, what Lauren was doing had nothing to do with him and everything to do with me—or so she had led me to believe at the time.

Standing there watching them together, I realized I was supposed to be scanning the joint for a lowlife. As I turned, a small waitress was looking up at me through large glasses.

"Can I help you, mister?" she asked.

"Where's the restroom?"

She pointed toward it, her eyebrows raised, even as her eyes narrowed. I had to walk right past it to get where I was now.

"Must've missed it when I came in."

"Must've," she said, then waited 'til I walked away.

Splashing some water on my face, I avoided the small mirror above the sink. I didn't need it to know that joining the dark circles and fine lines, the old desperation had returned. I could feel it. The last thing I wanted to do was see it.

As I looked away, patting my face, Ray walked through the door. At first, he looked surprised to see me, though I knew he had followed me out here, but then I saw what true surprise looked like when Harry Lewis walked in behind him.

"Well, Ray Parker," Harry said, grabbing his hand and giving it three good pumps, "how are you pal?"

How the hell do they know each other?

"Just fine, Mr. Lewis," Ray said, though at sixty he was nearly as old as Lewis. "How are you?"

"Be okay if I could get Howell off my heels," he said, making his way over to a toilet and unzipping his fly.

Harry's gray hair was thinner and more wispy than I remembered, and though his face had become pink and puffy, his eyes were just as blue.

"How is the race goin'?" Ray asked.

"Heatin' up," Harry said. "Heatin' up. I hope I can count on your support and . . ." He looked over at me.

"I'm sorry," Ray said. "This is my partner, Jimmy Riley. I don't think you ever met him."

Harry studied me for a moment and I felt like the sweaty, twitching guy in a police lineup.

His round face was spider webbed with broken blood vessels and deepening lines, and I wondered again what Lauren was doing with this sad old man.

But the truth was, I knew. It wasn't about money, though she spent a hell of a lot of it. It wasn't about fidelity. It wasn't that he was a good husband—he didn't act like a husband at all, but an indulgent grandfather. It had nothing to do with sex—according to her they hadn't had it in years. And even back when they did they never had much. It wasn't even about love, though I didn't doubt that they both loved each other as best they could. It was about loyalty, about what she thought she owed him, and maybe what she really did.

"No. I don't guess I ever did. Nice to meet you, Jimmy my boy. I'd shake your hand but mine's shaking my dick at the moment." Laughing, he turned back around to Ray. "I may have another job for y'all. Come by the bank one day this week or stop by campaign headquarters this weekend."

Just then a large man with a thick neck in a suit too small for him entered the tiny room a few minutes after his chest.

"Everything okay, Mr. Lewis?"

"Just fine, Walt. Just fine. Ray, Jimmy, this is Cliff Walton. He helps with security. Walt, this is Ray Parker and Jimmy . . ."

"Riley," I said.

"Riley, that's right. Ray used to work for the Pinkertons. They'll probably wind up helping us with certain matters before the campaign is over."

Walt wasn't happy to hear this, but only let it show a moment.

"They'll come in handy with Howell," Lewis added.

Frank Howell was Lewis's opposition in a closely contested mayoral race. Panama City's wartime boom with Tyndall Field, the naval section base, and Wainwright Shipyard made it a place of power, and both men hungered for piece of it—or maybe the whole damn pie.

A few minutes later when we walked out of the bathroom, Lauren was standing there waiting for Harry. I came out first and when she saw me, her eyes grew wide and alarmed, but quickly shrunk back into dark pools that lacked recognition as Harry appeared behind me.

"Darling, this is Raymond Parker and Jimmy Riley," Lewis said. "They may be helping with some security during the campaign."

She extended her hand to each of us and said, "I'm Lauren. It's nice to meet you."

"Haven't we met somewhere before?" I asked.

She had extended her right hand, and having to shake it with my left was awkward and unnatural. I gripped it tightly and didn't let go.

For just a moment she narrowed her eyes and pursed her lips, but then smiled and said, "I don't think so."

"Maybe you just have one of those faces," I said.

Instinctively, she reached up to ensure her hair was still covering her burns.

Pain and guilt gripped my heart. I hadn't meant her scars, and I felt sick to know she thought I had.

"That must be it," she said, her injured eyes glistening.

Harry was already chatting up another potential voter and missed most of what was going on between his wife and me.

"I didn't mean your—"

"Forget it," she said, shaking her head.

Ray grabbed me by the arm and began ushering me away.

"It was nice to meet you, *Mrs.* Lewis," I said.

Chapter 5

"Suppose you tell me how you know Harry Lewis," I said.

My voice was hard and flat, anger like static sizzling at its edges. I had never spoken to Ray this way before, but even if it got me canned on the spot, I couldn't stop.

"He hired me to follow his wife a while back."

"*When?*"

It wasn't so much a question as a demand. I was out of my precinct, and it'd probably cost me plenty, but I didn't care—never did when Lauren was involved.

"Eight months ago, a year, maybe. I'm not sure exactly. Not long after you got shot."

We were walking along the marina on St. Andrews Bay out behind the restaurant, the whish of the wind off the water, the metallic clanging of riggings, and the shrieks of gulls in our ears.

"I knew you'd worked for her before," he continued, "and I always suspected a personal relationship developed, so . . ."

Though old enough to be my dad—I was twenty-seven and he had to be nearly double that—Ray was the closest thing to a friend I had. His wisdom and insight had not only made me a better person, but saved me from more than a little self-destructive behavior. It's why I had kept Lauren from him. I hadn't wanted to be saved from her.

"So you took a case for *our* agency without *me* knowing," I said.

The truth was, it was Ray's agency. I just worked there. But I couldn't let a little thing like the truth get in the way of my outrage. I was sore as hell and had my cables all crossed up.

"I thought I was doing you a favor," he said. "You couldn't have worked it anyway, but the truth is, fella, you weren't in any condition to work anything at the time."

He was right. I hadn't been. It wasn't just my injuries either, my mind had jumped its rails. And the way I was handling all of this now showed how little that part of my condition had improved.

The rocking waters of the bay made a slapping sound as they struck the hulls of the boats moored in the marina. It was rhythmic, and provided a beat for our conversation.

"Why'd Harry want her followed?" I asked.

"Same as all the others. He thought the little woman was stepping out on him."

"Was she?"

"Why so anxious to dive off the dock for this dame, Jimmy? Maybe she's as swell as you think she is, maybe she ain't, but she ain't worth taking the big plunge for. No girl is."

I took in some air. It was acrid, thick with warmth and humidity, the sharp smell of fish and brine penetrating my nostrils.

"Was she?" I asked again.

"I don't know. Pulled me off the case before I had a chance to find out for sure. Said he was an old fool to have ever thought such a horrible thing about his little angel, but the next week he declared his intention to run for mayor, so . . . he gave us plenty of lettuce for our . . . ah, discretion, and you, me, and July haven't missed a meal since."

"You never saw her with anyone?"

"You gotta get clear of this thing my boy. I hate to see you—"

"Just keep dealing."

"The lady's careful. I didn't have time to find who was who and what was what before Harry put the kibosh on the whole operation."

I thought about it for a moment.

"What'd she want this morning?" he asked.

"To know if I'd been following her."

"Have you?"

"No."

"You think Lewis hired someone else?"

I shrugged. "Could be a jilted lover."

"Well, it's not our concern. You told her you couldn't take her case, didn't you?"

"No case. Just wanted to know if I was following her."

"So you two *were* . . ."

I didn't say anything.

"Jesus, Jimmy. Tell me you ain't gonna let some scarred-up two-bit broad that happened to marry well turn you all silly again."

I shook my head.

"You sure?"

"Her or any other," I said. "I'm impervious."

He raised his eyebrows and laughed. "All that reading's got you talking funny, fella."

"It's true," I said. "She's not a temptation. She's nothing."

"I don't want to lose you," he said, "but I can't afford to have some love-sick sap selling out my agency."

"Won't happen," I said.

"You sure? Sounds to me like she's still got her hooks in you but deep. Maybe you should take some time . . ."

My greatest fear was that Ray would let me go, that his charity would run out, he'd begin to see me as too much of a liability and give me the ole heave-ho, call me a casualty of a war I never got to fight in.

"Ray, I swear it," I said, sounding desperate. "Everything's jake. There's nothing—"

"I don't know. You sound a little too—"

"Listen to me, partner," I said. "It's not just that I won't do anything. I can't. I'm no use to women, and I got no use for them."

He smirked and let out a harsh little laugh. It said he knew better. "Now you're just bein' silly. Some time would do you good, soldier."

"No, really."

"Just looking out for you. Who else's gonna do it?"

I shook my head. I didn't want to have to tell him, not ever, but nothing else seemed to be working.

"Ray," I said. "I meant what I said. I'm impervious to women—especially Lauren Lewis. It's no good. Trust me."

"How can I? Look how you're already—"

"Because," I said, then paused to take a breath, "my arm wasn't the only thing injured when I got shot up."

Chapter 6

"I saw Lauren Lewis today," I said.

Ann Everett nodded slowly, and I could tell she was attempting to keep the concern out of her expression.

"It's a small town," she said. "I'm surprised it doesn't happen more often."

"We move in slightly different circles," I said.

She smiled.

Ann Everett didn't look like a psychologist—at least not how I pictured them. She reminded me of a co-star in a movie, attractive enough, but forgettable—a character actor, never a leading lady. She had short blonde hair, smallish green eyes, and black rimmed glasses.

When I had reached her office, a small house on Grace Avenue, I had asked her if we could take a walk, and we were now strolling around the quiet streets of downtown in the soft tea rose glow of evening.

"How'd you feel when you saw her?"

"I thought I wouldn't feel anything . . ."

"But you did?"

I nodded.

I was happy to be outside, away from her small office where we had discussed so many painful and shameful memories.

When I first came to her, shortly after getting shot, she had asked if she could record our sessions. She was doing a study about the effects of losing a limb on servicemen, and though I had been injured at home as a cop instead of overseas as a soldier, my experience was far more recent than most of the men she got the chance to interview. I had agreed, but always felt uneasy about it, and even after I quit the cops and she stopped making the recordings, I was never able to completely relax in that room.

"Do you mean . . ." She trailed off, and I saw her eyes move down my body.

I shook my head.

"Like what then?"

I thought about it, gauging how much I should reveal, the lies I was telling myself of far greater concern than any I'd tell her.

"I'm not sure."

"I know you, Jimmy. I know you've thought about it. Don't get cagey with me."

I didn't say anything.

The warm evening air was damp with moisture, and we both had a light sheen on our faces. Above us the Dixie Sherman, the only high-rise in the area, towered over all the other buildings, its form growing less defined against the darkening sky.

"I don't know. I felt a lot. I didn't write anything down."

"Where'd you see her? What happened?"

I told her.

"She hired you to find out who's following her?"

"No, I'm doing it as a friend."

"When'd you two become friends?" she asked.

"You know what I mean."

"No, I don't. She asked you as a friend?"

"No," I said, "but by making me aware of the situation she knew what I'd do."

"So she didn't ask you, but she wants you to?"

"You saying she doesn't?"

"I'm not *saying* anything. I'm *asking* you. What was it she said that made you think she wanted you to follow her?"

"She told me not to," I said.

In the distance, people stumbled out of a joint on the corner in a cloud of smoke, their loud voices and laughter startling in the quiet. From within, the faint, soothing sounds of the Andrews Sisters could be heard like the muffled music of a neighbor's radio.

"And that made you think she did?"

"You'd have to know her," I said. "She knew what she was doing."

"But do *you*?"

"She knew when she walked into my office that if she told me someone was following her I'd stop him."

"That may be, but I'm not concerned about her knowing what you would do as much as what you're doing and why you're doing it."

I had nothing for that.

"Is it possible she really did just think you were following her?"

I didn't say anything.

"You wanna save her or just be with her again?"

I looked at her, my eyes narrowing in anger.

"If you could," she said, "I mean *when* you can again—I know you'll be able to—would you want it to be her?"

I didn't want to think about any of that, didn't want to dissect what was really wrong with me—what was physical and what was psychological.

I glanced down at my watch. "I've got to go."

"Don't be sore, soldier. Suppose I didn't ask the difficult questions? What then? No one else in your life will."

"Don't call me that."

"I'm . . . I know how it makes you feel, but I meant it as a . . . you really do seem like a . . . it just fits you, fella."

I didn't say anything.

"It wasn't a crack. Don't let it distract from the real issue."

"I know what I'm doing," I said. "Everything'll be fine. After this, she'll be out of my life for good."

"Well," she said, her voice filled with an underlying gravity, "sounds like you're convinced."

"It won't be like before. Before . . . I carried a torch for her. I was a sap before. I can handle it now. Now, I'm nobody's sap."

Chapter 7

I was in my room in the Cove Hotel at Wilson Avenue and Cherry Street. It was a two-story Spanish-style hotel, surrounded by an Edenic landscaping of trees and flowers, with a dock and dive platform out into the bay. My room, which I could not have afforded otherwise, was part of my pay for being the house detective.

In the dream, we were lying in between sand dunes looking up at the stars, listening to the unseen waves of the Gulf caress the shore. Beneath us, the sand was cool, above us, the sky was dark and clear and dotted with stars, and around us, the beach was empty for miles.

Harry was at his weekly poker game, and we were whiling away the time as if we had it in such abundance we could never exhaust our endless supply.

Things were too good, too intense, and I needed her too much not to try to sabotage it all somehow.

"How long you think this'll last?" I asked.

"Don't," she said. "Not tonight."

"Every affair ends."

"I'm not going to let you spoil this. It's too perfect."

"I'm not trying to spoil it. I just—"

"Listen, soldier," she said. She called me soldier before I was wounded and everyone began assuming I was. "This is the big love for me. I'll never love another man. Not ever. This won't end for me—even if you end it. I'll still love you the way I've never loved anyone in my whole entire life."

"But—"

"Shut up," she said, placing her hand over my mouth, "and make love to me again."

The soft, incessant knock on the door brought me up out of the underworld, but as I stumbled toward the door, part of me remained submerged.

When I opened the door, Lauren rushed inside and closed it behind her.

In my groggy, half-conscious condition, I took her in my arms and kissed her hard on the mouth. At first she resisted, but then kissed me back, her body going limp into mine, my body responding to hers.

It wasn't until she pulled away that I became fully aware of the waking world I was in now, and realized that I didn't have two arms to wrap her up in and that my body couldn't respond to hers.

"I'm sorry," she said. "I didn't mean to—"

My shirt was off, my right shoulder and upper arm exposed. She stared at it, then at the other gunshot wound scars on my upper body.

I felt as exposed and as ugly as I ever had, but before I could make a move to get a shirt on, she took what was left of my arm in her hands and gently kissed it with her full, soft lips.

As she did, I felt my body responding to hers again, and realized that maybe it hadn't just been part of the dream. What was going on? How could I be . . .

The only time I had experienced anything like this before was last year while I was working a case for a woman who reminded me of Lauren. Like then, I wondered if this were some sort of phantom response, the way I could feel my right hand itching sometimes, or if I were experiencing the first faint flutterings of—what? Hope?

She looked down at the wrinkled mess of bed, at the books lining the spot where she used to lay after we made love, her moist body spent and emanating warmth.

"I'm sorry," she said. "I know it's late. I shouldn't have come, but someone's following me again and I didn't think you'd be here."

I stepped over to the chair beside my bed and wrestled my t-shirt back on, the heat of embarrassment like the sting from a slap on my face, realizing she was seeing how difficult this simple act was for me.

"You thought I'd be following you?"

"No," she said. "Maybe. I don't know what I thought. I was scared and I didn't know what else to do. I'm supposed to meet a man tonight to recover something of mine that was misplaced, but as I was leaving, I got the sense someone was following me."

"Recover something you misplaced?"

"Yeah. Why?"

"Who're you tryin' to kid, kid?"

"What?"

"You're forgetting who you're talking to," I said. "Reshuffle and deal again."

"You're right," she said. "The truth is, it was stolen and I'm paying to get it back."

"That's a little better, but not much. Go ahead, you can do it. Say the ugly little word."

"What?"

"Try the whole truth. It won't hurt as bad as you think."

"I'm tired, Jimmy. And I'm scared. I'm sorry I busted in on you like this, but I don't feel like fighting with you. I couldn't keep up."

"Who's blackmailing you, Lauren?"

"I'm going now. I'm glad it's not you who's following me. I really am. I actually thought you might still hate me so much that—"

"I don't blame you for what happened to me."

"I wasn't . . . I didn't mean . . . Why would you? How could I have—"

"It's nothing. Doesn't matter. Still loopy. Half asleep."

"No," she said. "I want to know. Have you forgotten I'm the injured party?"

"Interesting choice of words."

She shook her head. "I've got to go."

She turned to leave.

"Wait. You better let me tag along. Blackmailers really are the lowest sort."

Chapter 8

Lauren was right. Someone was following her. And he was very good. I became aware of him when we walked out.

"Go back to my room and lock the door," I whispered, then bolted after him.

He had been standing in a dark corner of the yard where the hedge met a group of palms, but by the time I reached it, he was gone.

I ran along the lit path around the hotel, guessing at the direction he was most likely to go, but stopped when I heard a car starting from beyond the tall, thick hedge row. I dove through the bushes, coming out the other side as he was racing away, and got a quick look at him before he disappeared into the night.

I was surprised at what I saw.

The man following Lauren wasn't a man at all, but a boy—at least he looked like one.

I retrieved Lauren, and we drove out to Panama City Beach toward the Barn Dance, a popular country and western dance hall, with our lights on low—a requirement during the war years.

I didn't ask her how she had enough fuel for the trip with the gas rations going on. There were only a few ways and I didn't want to hear about any of them—not about her husband's money or position, the way the rules for the rest of us didn't apply to them. Or worse, that she traded on her own assets in order to keep it from him. I really couldn't stomach a remark about her resourcefulness.

I looked over at her. "There *is* somebody following you."

"That's what *I* said."

"Well, you were right."

She turned in her seat and looked out the back window.

"Is he behind us now?"

I shook my head.

"He was outside the Cove."

"Thanks for coming," she said.

"Thanks for asking me," I said with a smile.

She laughed.

We were quiet a moment.

"I've missed you," she said.

I felt those same stirrings I had in my room.

"You realize what a mistake it was to leave me yet?" I asked.

She didn't say anything.

"I'm still not clear on why you did," I said.

She still didn't respond, and I regretted saying anything.

"It doesn't matter," I said. "We knew it would end eventually. I'm just sore I wasn't the one who got to fade first."

Built by local entertainer Neal McCormick, a radio performer who on occasion sang with Hank Williams, the Barn Dance was a wooden structure on Panama City Beach that resembled its name. It had regular Thursday and Saturday night dances and a separate restaurant and lounge that served food and drink.

When we pulled up in front of the vacant structure, my headlights illuminated the wagon wheels hanging on its wall and the painted sign that read: Barn Dance. Beneath it a smaller sign read: Cold Beer - Whiskey - Wine.

I fumbled in my coat for my small revolver.

"Who's blackmailing you and why?" I asked.

"Jimmy, I told you—"

"I need to know who we're dealing with. How dangerous they are."

"I'm supposed to go around back," she said, grabbing an envelope out of her purse and opening her door. "Wait here. I'll be right back."

"Sure, darling, I don't mind. I'm just the driver."

I cut the engine and got out, slipping my hand and the gun into the left pocket of my overcoat.

"I told you to—" she began.

"You've told me lots of things," I said. "And some of them actually turned out to be true, but Mrs. Riley didn't raise her sons to abandon ladies in desperate circumstances, no matter the kind of lady."

"Gee, but you've got a swell opinion of me," she said.

"Who you think gave me that?"

"If you only knew . . ."

"Only knew what?"

"Nothing."

"No, what?"

"I'll never be able to convince you, but I'm not the monster you think I am."

I thought about what she had said, but didn't respond.

We walked around the side of the wide wooden structure to the moonlit beach beyond, the sounds of the incoming tide and the shifting wind all I could hear.

It was dark and desolate, nothing but sand dunes and sea for as far as I could see.

"He a cop?"

I turned to see a kid stepping out from behind the opposite side of the barn, my eyes widening as I realized he was the same kid I'd just chased at the Cove. He was thin and boyish, and couldn't have stood more than about five and a half feet. He had wavy blond hair, pale, pubescent skin, and looked about fifteen, though he was probably nineteen or twenty. He held a large envelope in his small hand.

"He's not a cop," Lauren said.

His voice trembled a bit and his small body shook, but he seemed to relax a little when he saw I was missing an arm.

"What's he doing here?" he said.

"What were you doing outside the Cove half an hour ago?" I asked.

Lauren looked over at me, then back to him.

"You following me, Freddy?" she asked.

"Just to make sure you're okay."

"Then why'd you run?" I asked.

"'Cause someone was chasing me, mister," he said.

"Cute."

"I ain't no tough guy."

"Glad you cleared that up," I said. "Here I was thinkin' you were."

"Who is this guy, Mrs. Lewis?"

"He gave me a ride," she said. "That's all."

"And I wasn't the first or the last to do so, but I think I'm the one got taken for a ride."

"I meant out here. He drove me out here."

"Makes me a chauffeur," I said.

"Okay, Mrs. Lewis, I trust you," he said, "but don't make me sorry for doin' a good turn."

"I won't," she said. "You won't be. I promise."

He held up the envelope and began to move toward us. "Here's your—"

"I've got something for you, too," she said.

She took a few steps toward him. I stayed where I was, my hand still on the gun in my pocket. As they neared each other, I looked around the dark beach. There didn't seem to be anyone else around for miles.

"I told you I didn't want anything," he said. "What Rainer's doing to you is . . . I couldn't stand by and let him—"

"I know Freddy. You're okay. But this way you won't have to work for him anymore."

He handed her the envelope he was holding, but didn't take the one she was offering.

"Please," she said, extending it toward him even more. "For me."

"Okay, Mrs. Lewis," he said, taking the envelope on offer. "You know I'd do anything for you."

"Forget it kid," I said, though he was probably less than ten years younger than us. "She's way too big for you."

Lauren turned toward me, and even in the dimness I could see the anger in her eyes.

"Mrs. Riley teach her sons to make cracks like that in front of ladies?" she said.

As she did, Freddy took off, running back behind the side of the building he had emerged from.

I started after him, but she grabbed my arm.

"Take me home," she said.

I knew I should follow the kid. Maybe if I had, I could've kept him from getting himself killed—or at least seen who did so I could say so when I was accused, but as usual I did what Lauren wanted. I always did what Lauren wanted. Well, almost always. There was one exception. I never left her alone. Not for long anyway.

"Sure, Mrs. Lewis," I said, "you know I'd do anything for you."

Chapter 9

I was eating breakfast alone in the Lighthouse Café when the two cops walked in.

Standing at the entrance, they scanned the tables until they saw me, then walked over.

"Hi-de-ho, Jimmy," Pete Mitchell said.

Pete had been my last partner. He was a little younger than me with the clean-cut look of a cop and big bright eyes that appeared to have seen far less than I knew they actually had.

Both men wore black viscose suits, which had shrunk and looked uncomfortable. Viscose, which was made from wood pulp, was used when everything else was seized, limited, rationed, and restricted by the government, and, like rayon, which was also used a lot, was bad about shrinking. As if part of their uniform, they both had gray fedoras with black bands that looked nearly identical.

"Hi ya, Pete," I said.

He was trailed by an older man with a bit of the brawler about him—dark complexion, stubble, some scar tissue around his eyes, and a nose that had been broken more than once.

"This is my new partner, Butch Rowland," Pete said. "He just transferred up from Miami."

I nodded to Butch. He nodded to me. Neither of us said anything.

"Mind if we join you?" Pete asked, though Butch was already straddling a chair.

I swept my hand toward the table in a be-my-guest gesture.

Pete sat down, joining Butch.

"Don't have to ask what your *new* partner's up to," Pete said. "See the paper this morning?"

I nodded.

Ray was the key witness in the Hathaway case. Mrs. Hathaway wanted a divorce and had hired Ray to follow her oft straying husband. Mr. Hathaway hadn't wanted a divorce—at least not from Mrs. Hathaway's money, so he killed her.

Butch looked around the room, taking in the small café.

Located on the lower end of Harrison, the Lighthouse looked like a large milk bottle. It was early morning, and the place was hopping. Patrons, men mostly, crowded in around the tables, their coats and hats on the rack by the door. Over half the people in the joint had on uniforms, and everyone seemed to have an appetite.

I was nearly finished with breakfast—a wrecked Adam and Eve on a raft—so I ate the last corner of a piece of toast and pushed the plate away.

"Workin' anything interesting?" I asked Pete.

"And how. Caught a homicide this morning."

Almost involuntarily my eyebrows shot up. Even with all the changes the war was bringing to Panama City, there were still relatively few violations of the sixth commandment.

"I wish I had you on it," he said.

"Then we wouldn't have to ask you where you was last night," Butch said.

"*Me?*" I asked.

"I know it's screwy pal," Pete said, "but—"

"Who got rubbed out?"

"Us guys with the guns and badges ask the questions," Butch said.

"Butch," Pete said. "I told you. Jimmy's okay. Hell, he's a hero. He was one of us a year ago."

But not anymore, I thought. *Was* one of us meant I wasn't any longer. In his attempt to vouch for me, Pete had let me know how things stood. There was cops and there was everybody else, and I was just like everybody else now.

"Then he understands what we gotta do," Butch said. "How things gotta be."

"I was in my room," I said.

At nearby tables, people were still talking about how the Japs had recently executed one hundred American prisoners of war on Wake Island. They were gonna pay for what they done to "our boys," too, by God. Things would get squared all around.

"Who was killed?"

"Alone?" Butch asked.

"Most of the time," I said.

Might as well give myself a little maneuvering room. I might need it.

I looked at Pete, my eyes narrowed and intense. "Who was killed?"

"Kid named Freddy Moats," he said. "Know him?"

I looked up like I was thinking about it. After a moment, I shrugged. "Not sure," I said. "Who is he?"

"Nurse for some quack," Pete said. "Got a place on Eleventh Street. Calls it a sanatorium. Even got a patient or two."

"That help your memory any?" Butch asked.

I shook my head. "Still not sure. Met a guy named Freddy once, but I never caught his last name."

Butch smiled and nodded to himself as if he knew everything he needed to about me.

"So how'd I kill this guy?" I said.

"He was beaten to death," Pete said.

"By a one-armed assailant?"

"You can do plenty with that one arm, soldier."

Butch added, "What I hear, you'd'a killed the guy in the lobby of the Sherman the other day if your partner hadn't'a pulled you off him."

"You boys are serious," I said. "I must look pretty good for it if you're doing background on me."

"I'm a serious guy," Butch said. "And thorough. You should re-member that."

"I will," I said. "I'd write it down, but I'm right-handed."

"It's wanky, Jimmy," Pete said. "But you know how things work."

"No, but I'm finding it out," I said. "And quick."

"It's not like that, Jimmy," Pete said. "You gotta know I wouldn't—"

"What put you onto me in the first place? What's the connection between me and ole Freddy?"

"Got a witness," Pete said. "Now, I don't know how reliable she is, Jimmy, but she puts you with the victim last night not long before he was rubbed out."

"Witness got a name?"

"Yeah," Butch said, "her momma gave her one right after she was born. Just like mine. But you wanna remember the one mine gave me is Butch, not Dope."

Chapter 10

Walking back down Harrison toward our office, I spotted Cliff Walton, Harry Lewis's head of security, standing in front of the Ford place smoking a cigarette.

Smokes weren't rationed like sugar and gas and other things, but they were shipped overseas and given to soldiers. So they were tough to get. Still, most of the people I hung around had them. Must've been the company I was keeping.

When I neared the Tennessee House, he crossed the street and approached me.

"Riley, right?" he asked.

I nodded.

"I'm Walt," he said. "I work for Mayor Lewis."

"*Mayor* Lewis?"

"Will be soon," he said.

He withdrew a pack of Lucky Strikes from his coat pocket, shook one out, and offered it to me. I took it. He then pulled out a lighter and lit it for me.

"Thanks."

We stood in silence for a moment, watching the traffic on Harrison creep by, the morning sun glinting off the chrome and glass.

"Any idea where Mrs. Lewis is?" he asked.

I shook my head. "She's not at home or with her husband?"

"Mr. Lewis doesn't know where she is. She never came home last night."

My heart started racing and I could feel the panic inside begin. I took a deep breath and tried to slow my pulse and calm my center. I couldn't let anything show.

Last night when she told me to take her home I knew what she meant—back to town, not to her house. I wasn't allowed near her house, not even when we were together. I hadn't gotten her home last night, but I'd gotten her close. She'd dropped me off a block from her swanky domicile and I had walked back to the Cove. It was late. I was tired. It was a long walk. I thought I had done all I could to make sure she was safe. Guess I was wrong. Again.

"I'm sure you can imagine how sensitive this situation is. With the election coming up, Mr. Lewis can't afford any bad publicity."

I nodded.

Just down from us, in front of the Ritz Theater, a group of men and women in various uniforms were preparing for another war-loan drive. The army-air force were setting up an amphibious craft, called a "duck" on display, while the Easter Star and employees from Gulf Power and Commercial Bank were erecting poster-covered booths. Above them, the marquee of the Ritz read: Your war bond may be his ticket home.

"He'd like you to make a few discrete inquiries."

I looked at him. His neck looked too thick to say words like "discrete inquiries."

"Me?"

He nodded. "Your partner's gonna be tied up for a while with the Hathaway thing, ain't he?"

I nodded.

"No one can know," he said. "No one. This has to be on the QT. You're not working for Mr. Lewis. You're working for me. Communicate only with me. The race is too close. If Mr. Lewis's opponent or political enemies get anything they can use against him, he could lose the election. All I want you to do is find her and let me know where she is."

He paused for a moment, but I didn't say anything.

"Is Mr. Lewis justified in the trust he places in you?"

"I'll find her," I said.

"And?"

"No one will ever know I was even looking for her."

What was that about?" Ray asked.

I had taken only a few steps toward our office when he appeared beside me.

"What are you—"

"In recess," he said. "Judge had to hear an emergency petition in another case."

I nodded.

I knew I couldn't keep it from him. I just didn't know I'd be telling him so soon, but I really didn't have a choice now, and I wasn't going to lie to him.

"Mrs. Lewis is missing," I said.

"Since when?"

"She didn't come home last night."

As we talked, we walked past the Tennessee House and the Ritz Theater to our building, then up the stairs to our office. July wasn't at her desk and probably hadn't made it in yet.

"That's not much time," he said. "She could just be—"

"Someone she was with last night was found dead this morning."

He was about to sit down behind his desk, but stopped. "Who?"

"Kid named Freddy. May not be connected, but there it is. I'm gonna need a couple of days for this and maybe a little help from July."

He shook his head. "I'll find her. I'll take care of everything. You just—"

"Ray," I said. He stopped. I rarely used his name. "You can accept that I need to do this or you can accept my resignation."

For a long moment he didn't say anything, his face showing nothing as he considered me.

"That was kind of sudden," he said.

"I just wanted you to know how serious I am. I know you understand."

Before starting his own agency, before working for the Pinkertons, Ray was a tough Chicago cop, and though many years had gone by, a case from back then still haunted him.

Continually abused by her ex-husband, who repeatedly strolled right through his restraining order, Dorothy Powell was a victim in need of a hero—a role Ray was right for. Protecting her became an obsession for him. All but moving in with her and all but hospitalizing her ex, he lost his badge, his family, everything. But in the end, it was Dorothy Powell who suffered the greatest loss one of the few times Ray had not been around.

"Too well," he said.

"It's something I've got to do. Something I'm *going* to do one way or another."

He nodded.

"You'll be in court anyway," I said, trying to repair any damage.

"I always suspected she's the reason you lost your right jab," he said.

I didn't say anything.

He nodded to himself. "Be careful, Jimmy. And next time don't be so quick to offer your resignation. I might just feel like you're trying to push me around and take it."

Chapter 11

While July tracked down information on Freddy Moats and his boss,
Dr. Payton Rainer, I drove out to Lynn Haven, across the nearly
mile-long wooden bridge spanning North Bay, to Margie Lehane's
secluded clapboard house.

Margie, Lauren's childhood friend, liked her privacy, and she had
plenty of it. Her house was at the end of a winding dirt road and was
surrounded for miles on all sides by thick pine and hardwood forests.

I hadn't seen Margie since shortly before Lauren left me, and I
wasn't looking forward to the inevitable drama that waited for me
inside, but if Lauren was hiding, this was where it would be. It wasn't
because Lauren and Margie were close. They weren't, but they had
history, they understood each other, and Margie wouldn't ask any
questions.

I knocked on one of the glass panes of the large wooden door
and waited. I didn't have to wait long. She must have heard me pull
up in the yard.

She was wearing a blue silk housecoat, open to reveal much of
the blue silk gown beneath it, which was sheer enough to reveal much

of the body beneath it. Though it was only a little past eleven, she held a martini glass in her right hand.

"I knew you'd come back," she said. "I just didn't realize it'd take you so long. Some people are just slow learners."

She wasn't slurring her words yet, but it wouldn't be long.

"Look at that," she said, nodding toward my right coat sleeve, the bottom of which was pinned to the shoulder. "It's really gone."

"Most of it," I said. "Can I come in?"

She stepped aside and made an elaborate sweeping motion with her left hand.

I stepped inside and removed my hat.

"You did mean in the house?" she asked.

I let that one pass. It was okay. There would be others.

As we walked through the foyer and into the den, I looked around at the overly furnished rooms. Margie always had the latest and best and too much of it. Kroehler furniture, Nairn linoleum, Holmes Wilton carpets—I knew because she was always bragging about them. Like Lauren, Margie had married a man with money. Unlike Lauren, Margie had figured out a way to lose the man and keep the money.

"You wanna drink?" she asked, nodding toward the bar in the corner of the room.

As usual, Margie had the best-stocked bar around—Gilbey's and Dixie Belle gin, Seagram's Five Crown, Cobbs Creek, Mount Vernon, Paul Jones, and on and on.

"I'm okay."

"You want me to take your hat? Can't really do anything as long as you're using your one hand to hold your hat."

"Don't plan on doing anything."

Her face contorted into a narrowed, creased mask of anger and displeasure. "You always was a bastard, Jimmy, you know that?"

"You seen Lauren?" I asked.

"That's why you're here?" she said. "Sniffin' after her. Well, she ain't here. And I don't know where she is. And I wouldn't tell you if I did."

"Mind if I look around?" I said, already moving toward the other rooms.

"Yeah, I mind," she said, but she didn't follow me.

I searched the house. Her kitchen had brand new Formica countertops, a huge new Philco refrigerator, and a Western stove, though I'd never known her to cook.

Nearly every room had an abundance of items that were part of the ration, but I wasn't surprised. Things like rations didn't apply to people like Margie.

It didn't take me long to determine that Lauren wasn't in the house. Still, I lingered in the bedroom, among the Virginia House Hard Rock Mountain maple furniture Margie was so proud of. Several times she let me and Lauren use her bed when we needed a private place to be together—especially on those long mornings when Harry had board meetings.

Through the windows, I checked the backyard. Margie's car was the only one in it.

When I walked back into the livingroom, Margie had turned on her phonograph, removed her housecoat and gown, and was standing there completely naked except for the blue mules on her feet and the martini glass still in her hand.

"I know what you're really after, buster," she said.

I studied her body for a moment. It was something to see. "You've faired a lot better in the last year or so than I have."

"I don't mind you only got one arm, Jimmy boy," she said. "It's not really your arms I got much use for."

I shook my head, swallowing hard against a wave of nausea and guilt.

"You want me like before?" she said. "On the floor or bent over the davenport?"

When we were together, Lauren always used to say all she wanted was for me to be happy. Anytime I'd express jealousy about Harry, she'd laugh and tell me I had nothing to worry about from Harry. They didn't even sleep in the same room together anymore and hadn't had sex in years. He was like her father, but no matter what she said, I just couldn't stop obsessing. Finally, after she had had enough, and we could both feel our disintegration beginning, she said if it made me feel any better I could get a woman to sleep with when she wasn't around. All she wanted was for me to be happy. I was so torn up inside that she could be fine with me being with another woman, so convinced she didn't love me, not the way I loved her, that I took her at her word and fucked her friend. I did it to get her to react with the same jealousy and obsession I had, but she didn't have much of a reaction at all. She didn't leave me right away, and when she did, she said it had nothing to do with Margie, but how could it not?

Margie had placed her drink on the end table and was now bending over nearly touching her toes in front of me.

"Have you seen Lauren?" I asked. "It's important."

"Have you ever seen Lauren do this?" she asked, and began to touch herself.

"She's in trouble. If you know where she is, you need to tell me."

"Maybe your arm wasn't the only thing got blown off, soldier. That why Lauren left you?"

I pulled out one of my new cards and dropped it on the coffee table. "I've got a new number. Use it if you hear from Lauren. She's in danger. She needs help."

She picked up the card pushed it up inside herself.

"Lauren's not the only woman who needs a private dick now and again."

I shook my head, as much at myself as her, wondering how I could have been such a sap. "The drunker the floozy," I said, "the blunter the patter."

Driving back into town, I thought about Lauren and wondered where she was and what she was up to. I should've forced her to show me what she bought from the kid, made her tell me what she was mixed up in and with who, and insisted I take her home, but as usual I had gone soft. I had been confused by her lies, intoxicated by her Paris perfume, and once again I was playing the sap for her.

We had it good for a while. Real good. Maybe that's why I couldn't let go, why I couldn't stop acting her fool.

As I drove through Lynn Haven, I remembered riding back from Margie's with Lauren after one of our mornings together. As usual, it had been so good that it scared me, and I was trying to pick a fight with her.

"Why won't you leave him?" I asked.

"I can't."

"You won't. There's a difference."

"I love you more than I've ever loved anyone—ever *will* love anyone," she said, "but I can't leave Harry."

"Then you love him more."

"It's not love," she said. "It's something else."

"Whatever it is, it's stronger than what you have for me."

"It's not. You know it's not."

"You're choosing him over me."

Even in the midst of acting like I was, saying the things I was, I'd tell myself to stop, attempt to gather some self-respect and regain some self-control, but I couldn't, and I hated her for what I'd become.

"Please don't see it like that," she said. "It's not like that at all. I just owe him so much. I couldn't do that to him."

I knew what she owed him. Her life.

Shortly before his death, Coolidge Brown, Lauren's father, Harry's best friend and the vice president of Harry's bank, had used his position of trust to provide reckless and unsecured loans for friends and embezzled a small fortune for himself. When Harry discovered what he was doing, he confronted him, demanding his resignation and threatening to squawk.

Secretly consumed with envy, Coolidge invited Harry over to his home ostensibly to apologize and discuss restitution, but really to take Harry down with him and his family. At gunpoint, Coolidge set his house on fire, dousing his wife, his kids, and his boss with kerosine. Not only had Harry acted bravely and saved Lauren's life, but he also covered her dad's crimes with his own money, burying the scandal with him. He provided for Lauren through high school and even some college, eventually asking her to take the place of his deceased wife.

"You're not even like a wife to him," I said. "He wouldn't mind so much."

"The only thing he's ever wanted in his whole life is to be in public office. If I left him what chance would he have? I can't do that to him. Can't deny him the one thing in all the world he wants."

"No?" I said. "Well, you sure don't have any problem doing it to me."

Nearing Panama City now, I thought about how I had actually believed her. I thought she really did love me the way she said, thought she just honestly couldn't bring herself to leave Harry. I thought all this right up until the moment she told me it was over.

Chapter 12

Dr. Payton Rainer had his office in a converted hotel on Eleventh Street near St. Andrews. Standing two stories, it had a courtyard in the back and was surrounded by a cement privacy wall on all sides.

When I rang the bell next to the locked front gate, a large man in a gray suit came out to greet me.

"Can I help you, sir?" he asked.

"I'd like to see Dr. Rainer," I said.

"Do you have an appointment?"

I shook my head.

"Then, I'm sorry, sir, but that's quite impossible."

"That I don't have an appointment?"

"That you could ever see Dr. Rainer without one," he said.

"Tell him I'm a friend of Freddy's."

"Freddy no longer works here, sir."

"On account of he's dead," I said. "I know. That's why I want to talk to Rainer."

"If you wish to wait, I'll check with Dr. Rainer," he said.

"I don't wish to wait," I said. "I wish to be inside, but if I have to wait I wish not to wait long."

He walked back inside and I waited. Contrary to my wish, I had to wait a while.

The traffic on Eleventh was steady in both directions, Fords mainly, but a few Pontiacs, Packards, and Oldsmobiles mixed in.

A few of the people riding by saluted me, others yelled things like, "Thank you for what you did, buddy."

I laughed and shook my head. I knew patriotism was high, but so was stupidity.

That was low—and it wasn't true. They didn't mean anything but good will. I was just sore, sick of being less than what people assumed.

When the big man finally returned, he was not alone. He was accompanied by an average-sized man he made look small, who wore a white lab coat and had a stethoscope hung around his neck. His skin was the color of tea stains and he had black eyes and black wavy hair.

Though his nationality was indeterminable, he looked foreign, and my guess was he'd talk with an accent, his degree in medicine, if he had one, wouldn't have come from the states, and Payton Rainer wouldn't be the name his mama gave him.

Both men stopped a few feet from the gate.

"May I help you, sir?" he asked.

He spoke with an accent, but I couldn't figure out what kind it was.

"You Dr. Rainer?" I asked.

"I am."

I handed him my card through the bars of the gate. The big man stepped forward, took it, and handed it to him. He glanced down at it and when he looked up again, his demeanor had changed.

"Then I'd like to come in and talk to you about Freddy."

"I'm afraid I can't let you in," he said. "We have patients with very sensitive conditions. No one is allowed in."

"What kind of doctor are you?" I asked.

"The same kind of detective you are," he said. "Private."

"What kind of medicine do you practice?"

"I heal the whole person," he said. "Spirit, mind, and body. They're all connected, you understand."

"Any idea who killed Freddy Moats?"

"That is a matter for the police," he said.

"What do you have on Mrs. Lewis?"

"I don't understand the question," he said.

"Is she a patient of yours?" I asked, surprising myself by my ability to use the term "patient" without busting up.

"I cannot confirm or deny if someone was a patient," he said.

His use of the word "was" wasn't lost on me.

"I'm afraid I really must return to my patients."

"Is Mrs. Lewis inside there right now?" I asked.

"Good day, Mr. Riley," he said, bowed his head slightly, and turned and walked away.

And there was nothing I could do about it. The gate was too solid, and the wall too high for a right-handed man who only had his left.

Chapter 13

I walked down the block to a Gulf service station and called Pete Mitchell at police headquarters. He wasn't in, but when I gave the desk sergeant my name, he took down the number and my location and said he'd have Detective Mitchell call me right back.

He did.

"Jimmy?"

"Yeah?"

"Where are you?"

I told him.

"Stay there," he said. "I'm on my way."

I hadn't even told him what I needed his help with.

When Pete and Butch pulled into the parking lot of the service station in their black Ford, they were followed by a black and white patrol car. Pete looked worried. Butch looked happy.

Butch rolled down his window. "Get in," he said.

Looking past him at Pete, I said, "I need your help. I think Rainer has—"

"Jimmy," Pete said. "Get in the car."

I took a breath and tried to calm myself.

The two men in the car looked like complete opposites. Pete, with his bright, clear blue eyes, had a face that was boyish and open. Butch, his dark eyes hooded and wary, had a face with a hard history etched into it.

"What's with all the orders, boys?"

"There's two ways we can do this," Butch said.

"Yeah?" I said. "Can I guess what they are?"

"Jimmy, it's me, Pete, your old partner," he said. "Just trust me and get in the car."

I got in the backseat.

"What's going on, Pete?" I asked.

Butch said, "You tell us."

"What are you mixed up in, Jimmy?" Pete asked.

"Not much at the moment," I said. "I'm—"

"Why'd you kill her?" Butch asked.

My heart seemed to stop beating, my suddenly cold blood standing still inside my veins. *Lauren's dead and they think I killed her.*

"Hey Pete," Butch said, "your old partner don't look so good, does he?"

"Take it easy, Butch," Pete said.

"You better not throw up in our car," Butch said.

I calmed myself, focusing my attention on the anger I felt at Butch, determined not to let him rattle me.

"Who'd I kill this time?" I asked. "I forget."

"Come on, Jimmy," Pete said, "don't be sore. We're just doing our jobs."

"Who's dead?" I asked, my voice flat, demanding.

"As if you don't know, you sick fuck," Butch said.

"Margie Lehane," Pete said.

"Yeah," Butch said, "and we found your card inside her pussy."

Like Margie herself, her place had been ravaged. Her killer had obviously been searching for something. Every room in the house had drawers open, their contents spilling out, overturned furniture, ripped and torn pillows, cushions, and mattresses, emptied closets, and opened books.

"Wonder if he found what he was looking for?" I asked.

"You tell us," Butch said.

The livingroom was like all the others, except that joining the other items on the floor was the naked body of Margie Lehane. She had been beaten, but good, especially her face, which was unrecognizable. Her beauty-shop blonde hair had blood-red highlights, two of her teeth had been knocked out, and judging from the positions they were in, at least one of her arms and one of her legs was broken. Her blue gown and housecoat were still draped over the arm of the davenport. One of her mules was still partially on her foot, the other on the floor about a yard away.

Her phonograph was still on. It was playing Tommy Dorsey's "I'm Getting Sentimental Over You."

As I stood there taking everything in, Butch came up beside me.

"You must have ice water in your veins," he said.

I didn't say anything.

"How can you just stand there admiring your handiwork without it bothering you the least little bit?" he asked. "How could you even do that to a dame in the first place? I mean that Freddy faggot was one thing, but how could you do this to her?"

I nodded. "That's a good question," I said. "How could I?"

At first he didn't get what I meant, but a moment later, his eyes widened slightly in comprehension.

"How could a guy with one arm—not his good arm at that—do all this?" I held up my left hand, made a fist and showed it to him. "Where's the blood, or bruising, or at least swelling?"

"Who's helping you?" he asked. "He's turnin' on you, stickin' your card inside her like that."

I turned to Pete. I was surprised he wasn't saying more. "You think the same person killed Freddy?"

"They were both beaten to death," he said. "Ain't somethin' you see every day. Plus, they both got a connection to you."

"Pete," I said, "you even entertaining the possibility I did this?"

"How'd she get your card up her . . . you know, inside her?"

I told them—about being here this morning, about giving her my card, and what she had done with it. The more I talked, the more worried Pete looked.

"That don't tell us why you was here," Butch said. "Or who you was working for."

"I'm lookin' for someone," I said. "I thought Margie might know where the person is."

"Who?"

I shook my head.

Butch let out a harsh, humorless laugh and shook his head.

"Did she?" Pete asked.

"Said she didn't, but I don't know."

"And when you left, she was alive?"

"When I left, she was naked and had just stuck my card inside herself, she was drinking a martini, and without even trying she was breathing in and out all on her own."

"Wonder what the guy was looking for?" Pete asked, then turning to me added, "Any ideas?"

I shook my head. "Sorry I can't be more help boys, but I didn't have anything to do with it, so I don't know anything."

Butch was rubbing his crooked nose with his index finger. He did that a lot when he wasn't busy terrifying me.

"What happened to you?" Butch asked. "Pete says you was a good cop. What made you so bent? You bitter—mad at the force 'cause you lost your arm and got canned? That it?"

I didn't say anything.

"Withholding information from real cops is a crime," he said.

I still didn't respond.

"You better watch your step, gumshoe," he said. "Just 'cause you maybe didn't do this don't mean you can't go down for it."

I looked over at Pete. "Things have changed a lot since I left," I said.

"Not so much, Jimmy," he said. "He's just saying we know you know more than you're telling us and we don't like it none."

"Well, you don't have to," I said. "I wouldn't like it either, and maybe I's you I'd keep an eye on me, but I wouldn't set up an innocent man, not if he was my worst enemy."

"Well," Butch said, "that's the difference in you and me, and I's you, I'd keep that in mind."

Chapter 14

When we stepped out onto Margie's porch, Butch waved one of
the uniformed officers over. "Take Mr. Riley back into town for me,
would you?"

"I'll do it."

We all turned to see Frank Howell, the current mayor and Harry's
opposition, walking toward us. A large man in every way, Howell was
tall and thick bodied, his fleshy face tanned, the center of his cheeks
pocked with acne scars.

The yard was filled with Panama City Police and Bay County
Sheriff's Deputy's cars, an ambulance, and a couple of reporters.
Howell had stepped out of the crowd.

Howell had an odd walk for such a large man. It was light-footed
and feminine, and looked to be the walk of a former dancer.

"Mr. Mayor," Pete said. "We'll take him. We didn't mean—"

He shook his large head. "I need to speak with Mr. Riley," he
said. "This'll give us the chance." He turned and looked at me. "That
okay with you?"

I nodded.

"I would ask you boys what you've got in there and how it's going," Howell said, "but it's out of my jurisdiction and I don't want to appear to be overstepping my bounds."

As we talked, a cameraman with one of the reporters snapped our picture. I attempted to position myself so I could use Howell for cover, but the photographer just continued altering his angle.

"Well, thank you, Mr. Mayor," Pete said. "That will let us keep working our investigation." He turned to me. "And Jimmy, don't you worry about anything. We'll get this all straightened out real soon."

As Howell and I walked away, the reporters shouted a couple of questions at us. I ignored them, and to my surprise, Howell did too.

We got into the back of his large red Packard Clipper and the driver eased out of the yard back onto the dirt road.

Though it had been Howell who honored me with a ceremony after I was shot, pinning the commendation on my coat himself, we had never spoken, and I had always thought the presentation was far more about a photo op for him than anything having to do with me.

"I hope our officers didn't go too hard on you," he said.

I shook my head.

"Hero last year, homicide suspect this year," he said. "It's amazing how quickly things change."

I nodded.

"And how quickly people forget," he added. "You're one of the few bonafide non-war heroes we have around here. How can they possibly think you're capable of what was done to that poor girl?"

The enormous backseat of the Packard was made more so by the double recessed front seats. I had seen houses with less head and leg room. Of course, a guy the size of Howell could use it. It probably didn't seem roomy to him at all.

"You know why politics are so dirty?" he asked.

"The people they attract?" I said.

He smiled, his enormous face spreading even more.

"I think you're being set up," he said. His voice matched his build. It was deep sounding and forceful even when he was speaking softly. "Are you working for Mr. and Mrs. Lewis?"

I didn't answer.

"I don't expect you to divulge the names of your clients," he said, "but if you are, be careful. Harry Lewis will stop at nothing to be mayor of our city, and with all the growth and changes—the military bases, the shipyard, the government contracts, the real estate boom—well, in the wrong hands a lot of bad things can happen."

He paused, but I didn't say anything.

"Harry's up to something," he said. "He may be using his wife and some quack named Rainer—calls himself a doctor. I just hope he's not using you."

"No one's using me," I said, as if I actually believed it.

"Glad to hear it," he said. "I just hope you'll keep it that way."

"I will."

"The reason politics are so dirty," he said, "is because there's so much at stake. Now, I'm no saint, and I'm not saying I am, but I'm not tempted by money and power. I have all I need of both of them. I don't see the mayor's office as a stepping stone to county, state, or national positions. I love Panama City. It's my home. My family helped to build it. And right now it's going through the biggest and most important changes it ever will. It's no exaggeration to say our small town can actually win or lose the war. That's what people like Harry Lewis don't get. They're too busy planning their next move, they don't see the damage their self-interests are doing."

The driver turned off Highway 231 onto Harrison.

Howell withdrew a card from his vest pocket and handed it to me.

"You may not know it yet," he said, "but we have the same enemies. My home number is on this. If you need me for anything, you be sure to let me know."

I nodded. "Thanks," I said.

The driver pulled the big Packard up in front of our office door, Howell and I shook hands, mine momentarily disappearing in his, and I got out. As soon as the door was closed, he rolled down the window.

"Oh, and Jimmy," he said, "as long as I'm mayor you will not be harassed by the police or set up for murders you didn't commit."

He didn't say it, but the implication was clear. It was in my best interest to do what I could to help keep him mayor.

Chapter 15

The next morning, July walked into my office and dropped the *Herald Tribune* on my desk. I looked down at it. There I was on the front page right next to the latest war news, above the fold, surrounded by police in front of Margie's house. The headline read: Former Detective Suspect in Murder of Local Socialite.

"When you get mixed up in something, you don't do it by halves, do you, soldier?" she said.

I smiled at her, but only a moment, as I quickly scanned the article.

"Does Ray know what you're involved in?"

Nodding to the paper on my desk, I said, "It looks like all of Panama City does now."

"Anything in it?"

"You asking if I killed Margie Lehane?"

"No," she said. "You didn't, did you?"

"Has Ray made it in yet?" I asked.

She shook her head. "He may be going straight to the court-house. I'm not sure. You know how he is. What's that word you used?"

"Taciturn."

"You gotta get a girl, fella," she said. "That ain't even the word you used last time."

I smiled.

"He never tells anybody much," she said. "Tells me even less."

"Why you think?" I asked, though I knew. I just wondered if she did.

"Because I'm not a . . . a . . . peer—not that Ray really has any of those. I'm more a project. Speaking of . . . he had an old file open on his desk yesterday."

"Dorothy Powell?"

She nodded. "She haunts him, but good, don't she?"

"If you're a savior, the ones you don't save always do."

"You two aren't alike in a lot of ways, but in that you are."

I wondered what she meant, but I didn't ask her. I didn't have to. She went on to tell me.

"Someone needs savin'—especially a woman, you two are the first guys to step forward, and you feel completely responsible for her the rest of your lives. It's the way Ray is with me, and you are with Lauren Lewis."

It wasn't quite the same with Lauren, but before I could say so, two men walked through my door without knocking.

The first man was small and thin, probably nearing middle age, well dressed and smooth. The man who followed him was his mus-cle—big, bulky, powerful. I had seen and dealt with enough men like them to know the sort of men they were. They were here to deliver a threat, issue an ultimatum, give a warning. They were the kind of men who if you saw a second time meant someone was getting hurt or dead.

The big man would have no problem tossing me around the room with one hand, snapping me in two with so little effort it wouldn't raise his heart rate, but the little one was by far the more dangerous of the two. I knew it before he opened his mouth, before he delivered a single threat or made good on it. I could see it in his eyes. It wasn't what was there, but what wasn't. Behind his gray eyes there was no conscience, no empathy, no pity, no mercy, no remorse.

The smaller man sat down in one of the chairs in front of my desk.

"Excuse us a minute, doll," he said to July.

She started to protest, but I shook my head, and she walked out quietly and closed my door.

"That was smart, soldier, you got brains," the small man said. His voice was low and flat, with only occasional inflection. "No need to get the pretty girl mixed up in any of this."

The small man had a grayish tint to him. Perhaps it was that his gray pinstripe suit and gray felt fedora matched his eyes. Maybe it was the faint gray stubble on his face, but it seemed to be more than that, as if his little body put off the color of his core somehow.

"Any of what?" I asked.

The big man, who wore a slightly too-small black suit, remained standing and had yet to make a sound or an expression.

"Complicated things like politics, medical treatment, and romance," he said. "Things guys like us should stay out of."

"Brother, I'm about as far out of those things as a body can be," I said. "Got no political interests—let alone aspirations, got no use for women, and not undergoing any medical treatment."

"Not yet," the big man said.

He sounded like a slow, mean kid, and I wondered how the little man put up with him.

"Must be tough havin' only one arm," the little man said.

"There're worse things," I said.

"Sure, soldier, but you're in the tough-guy business," he said. "Hard to be tough with only one arm."

"I do all right," I said.

"I'm sure you do," he said. "But goin' up against the locals what pass for muscle around here's one thing. Takin' on guys like us is another."

"Maybe," I said. "Doesn't change anything, but it may be true."

"Okay, soldier, I understand," he said. "I'm just wasting my breath here. Doesn't matter what I say, we're gonna mix it up 'cause that's what guys like us do, but I still gotta give you the message I's hired to just like there was a chance you might actually listen to it."

I nodded.

"Man who hired me thinks it's best you stay out of politics, away from other men's wives, and away from hospitals."

The big man came to life again, his face showing his pride in himself and the pleasure what he was about to say would bring him. "If you don't," he said, "you'll need a doctor and a hospital of your own."

"But not a politician or another man's wife?" I asked.

The big man looked confused. The small man smiled.

"You ought not do that, mister," the small man said. "That's just low."

"According to you, I'm gonna have a short life," I said. "Better get my fun while I can."

Chapter 16

It cost me extra, but I had Clipper in a uniform. He was banging on the delivery entrance of Rainer's place on Eleventh Street, a brown parcel in his left hand. A single-bulb light fixture above the door provided the only illumination, and from my position in the back of the delivery truck all I could see of him was his white uniform, the white of his real eye, and his bright white teeth.

Clipper Jones was a young Negro who had been part of the 99th Fighter Squadron, 1st Tactical Unit before suffering the loss of his left eye. He picked up the nickname Clipper while training at Dale Mabry Field because of the way he would so fearlessly dive down toward the Gulf, fly in low and "clip" the tops of the north Florida pine trees.

The back door of the private sanatorium opened, and Clipper began his routine.

I was crouched in an old milk truck. One of Clip's many brothers had converted it into a delivery vehicle. I was attempting to see and hear what was going on near the door.

"He's not here," the dark-haired nurse said.

It had rained earlier in the night and was threatening to again. The air was thick with moisture. As if steam rising out of the earth from small hidden holes, a low fog hovered over the ground, some of it breaking free to cling to tree branches and gather itself around the lights on buildings and street corners.

"This here's gots to be signed fo," Clipper said. "And it's gots to be Dr. Rain to do it."

"Rainer," the woman corrected.

"Rai-n-er," he repeated slowly.

I thought he was overdoing it a bit, but he often told me you could never overestimate the superiority white people felt over coloreds.

He must have been right because of what she did next.

"Come in," she said. "I'll call Dr. Rainer."

She turned and began walking inside. Before he followed her, Clipper looked back in my direction and gave me a big, fuck-crackers smile, which was about all I could see.

When Dale Mabry Field near Tallahassee was expanded from a small airport used by private planes, Eastern Airlines' DC3s, and National Airlines' mail carriers to an Army airfield in late 1940, a small black community had been relocated. Clipper's grandparents had been part of this community. It had never set well with Clipper, and he didn't mind letting his superiors know it. In fact, his antics in the airplane that earned him his nickname were part of his protest. He had always suspected his eye injury wasn't an accident—hired me to prove it, but I couldn't get past the army's tall green wall of silence and endless miles of red tape.

Within a few minutes, Clip was opening the back door and waving me in with the gun in his right hand. I climbed out of the truck and joined him.

"Not much security," he said. "One fat fucker I slapped the shit out of."

"Where's the nurse?"

He jerked his head toward the open door. "Come see for your-self."

I followed him into a tile-floor lobby to find the discarded box his gun had been in, the fat security guard on the floor, and the night nurse cuffed to a big wooden chair, a piece of tape across her face holding a gag in her mouth.

"Why the gag?"

"Take it off and see," he said. "Shit, Jim, how long it gonna be 'fore you quit questioning every got damn thing I do?"

I started to remove the gag, but stopped myself. "Sorry," I said.

The small lobby had brownish linoleum with green-and-rust-colored frames around Oriental rugs. A reception area behind a small glass sliding door stood on one wall, the light inside it providing the only illumination for the dim lobby. In the middle of the open space, two seating areas, one a modern Kroehler couch and chairs, the other East Indies Rattan.

Off the lobby in opposite directions, two corridors extended about a hundred feet with doors on each side.

"We just gonna bang on every door until we find her?" he said.

Lightening flashed outside and for a moment the entire room was bright and well lit. A few seconds later thunder rolled in the distance. Another storm was moving in off the Gulf.

I shook my head. "I'm gonna quietly look for her. You're gonna stay here and keep an eye on things."

The hallway was dim, lit only by intermittent fancy fixtures with low-watt bulbs inside them. Several rooms were empty, the beds made, the doors open. I tried the handle of the first closed door I came to. It was unlocked. I opened it. Inside, I found a tall man with a long white beard sleeping on his side. I closed it and tried the next one. This time I found a rotund woman lying on her back, a small dog asleep on her slowly rising and falling chest.

I had gone through a handful of rooms when I found Lauren's. She was fully dressed, sitting on her bed, crying.

"Jimmy," she said, as she jumped off the bed, rushed over, and hugged me.

"You okay?" I asked.

"What are you doing here?"

"Came for treatment," I said. "Whatta you think?"

"I can't go," she said.

"I'm not giving you a choice."

Lightening flashed outside, illuminating the raindrops on her window.

"You don't understand," she said.

"Well, you can explain it to me or keep me in the dark," I said. "Either way you're coming with me."

She didn't say anything.

"You want to tell me what's going on?" I asked. "What does Rainer have on you?"

"Nothing," she said.

I shook my head. "There was a time when you told me everything," I said. "At least I thought you did. Was I wrong about that, too?"

The wind picked up and pelted the window with a volley of raindrops. Through the rain-spattered glass pane I could see the leaves of banana trees and palm fronds waving in the wind.

I could tell she wanted to change the subject. She said. "If you're forcing me to go, we better get going."

Chapter 17

"Clipper?" Lauren asked. "What're *you* doin' here?"

"Ever since your soldier here done got hisself shot up, he can't do shit by hisself."

I laughed, but only so they wouldn't see the sick look on my face. He was right. There were many aspects of my job and my life I could no longer do, and though there wasn't anything I could do about it, I wasn't about to get used to it.

"Would you please tell him I need to stay here," she said.

He looked confused. "You don't want to go?"

"No," she said. "I can't."

Lightening flashed and lit up the room, Lauren's eyes growing wide at the sight of the bound and gagged nurse and unconscious security guard.

"You don't have a choice," I said. "Let's go."

"You heard the man," Clip said. "He da one puttin' money in my pocket tonight."

As we walked out, Lauren looked back at the night nurse with an expression of helplessness and apology. "Tell Dr. Rainer I was forced to leave against my will. I'll be back. And I'll pay him every penny. Okay? Got that? Be sure to tell him."

The nurse nodded.

We continued moving, Lauren leading, and I realized Clip had stopped. I turned to make sure he wasn't about to shoot the nurse or night watchman, and found him leaning over saying something to the nurse.

When he reached me, I asked him what he had said to her.

"That I put the key to the cuffs in fat boy's shirt pocket so he can free her when he wake up."

"That was nice," I said.

"She ain't bad lookin'," he said. "Still want a white woman—least once."

"Oh," I said, with a big smile. "So you were being romantic."

"Well, I can't just break in and kidnap a dame," he said. "I ain't that romantic, but—"

Lauren had already stepped out of the back door and she was now coming through it again, a gun held to her head by the small gray-tinted man who had been in my office earlier in the day. He was standing behind her, using her body as a shield. The big man was behind him. I could see his upper body and head over Lauren and the little guy. He had to duck to walk through the door.

Through the door behind them, I could see that the rain was coming hard now, slanting in the wind, visible in the light mounted beside the door.

When I looked back at Clip, he was pointing his gun at them.

"Tell the nigger to drop the heater, soldier," the little gray man said to me.

They were inside now. The big man had his gun out too, pointing it at me.

I looked at Lauren, trying to reassure her, to let her know everything was okay, though clearly it was not.

She said, "Looks like you showed up for a gun fight with only your fists."

"One fist at that," Clip said. "Ain't that some kind of shit."

"I said tell your nigger to drop his gun," the small man said.

Lightning flashed, followed fast by a sharp clap of thunder. The storm was on top of us now.

"He think you pay me enough for me to be your nigger?" Clip asked.

"I do pay you a lot," I said.

"Not enough to be your nigger," he said. "Nobody got *that* much money."

"Okay, fellas," the little man said, "I've let you have your fun. Now drop the gun or Mrs. Lewis here's gonna have something even Dr. Rainer can't help her with."

"I ain't never put down my gun for no man," Clip said. "Never goin' to neither."

I knew that was the case, which was why I had been stalling. Clip would die before he'd relinquish his weapon. It was a matter of pride, a defiance that preferred death to dishonor, which was how he viewed surrendering in any form. It was what made him so dangerous, but in this instance he was endangering Lauren's life, and I was the one who had set it up.

"You better talk to him, soldier," the little man said to me. "He's gonna get the lady killed."

"He won't put down his gun," I said. "Not for any reason. He'll die first. Let us all die."

"You be the first one I shoot," Clip said to the little man.

"So we know Mrs. Lewis will die and we think perhaps I will," the little man said. "Wonder who else will? Mountain, who you gonna shoot first?"

"Got my gun on the cripple, Cab," Mountain said.

"He's got no gun and one arm, Mount," Cab said. "Why don't you point it at the jig."

As Mountain moved his gun off me, Clip shot him in the face. He dropped his gun as he was falling and I picked it up.

"Look like the crip and jig got the drop on you," Clip said.

The thunder and lightening were happening nearly simultaneously now, the flashes of light and cracks of sound so often as to be almost continuous.

"I've still got the girl," Cab said.

His voice was much softer now and not nearly as confident. He hadn't expected what had just happened, and wasn't quite sure what to do.

"Mrs. Lewis and I are going to back out of here," he said, "and you two are going to let us. I know you'll shoot me now, so I won't hesitate to shoot her."

He began backing out, dragging Lauren with him. Clip and I began to follow.

"Stop right where you are," he said. "Or I'll shoot her right now."

"Then get shot yourself," Clip said.

"I don't mind dying so much," he said.

When they reached the back door and he had stepped through it, Lauren's heel got caught on the threshold and she tripped and fell. As she was going down, Cab released her, fired off a few rounds at us, and disappeared into the rainy night.

I ran over to Lauren. Clip ran past us out into the storm in search of Cab.

"Are you okay?" I asked.

The security guard was beginning to stir and the doors of patients' rooms were opening. In another moment we'd have a crowd of eyewitnesses.

"I'm better than Mountain," she said, nodding to the large man lying on the floor, an expanding pool of blood beneath his head.

"I'm glad," I said. "Let's get out of here."

I helped her up, then checked outside. Clip ran up just then. He was soaked through, his face and hair dripping.

"I missed him," he said. "He's gone."

"We'll deal with him later," I said. "Let's get Lauren home."

"Whatta you mean *we'll?*" he asked.

"That I'll—"

"That cracker's all mine," he said.

Chapter 18

"What are you mixed up in, Lauren?" I asked.

She didn't say anything.

I took my time driving Lauren home, using the hard slanting rain and wet streets as an excuse, but it didn't do any good. Every attempt I made to start a conversation failed. I was trying to remind her of how good it had been between us, convince her she could still trust me, but she just wouldn't respond.

I changed my approach.

"Does Harry know?"

"No," she said. "He has nothing to do with this."

Still protective over Harry.

"It's a private matter," she said.

"Not any more it's not," I said. "People are dying. That kind of thing always draws attention. Pesky cops and reporters are gonna keep at it until they have something."

"But it was self-defense," she said, and I wasn't sure I wanted to hear the rest. "I'll swear to it. Nobody's gonna—"

"Who was self-defense, Lauren?"

"The big guy Clipper shot tonight," she said. "He won't get in any trouble for that, will he? Even if he does, I'll testify my life was in danger and he saved me. It'll just have to be after the election is over."

The storm was continuing to move past us, the thunder and lightning nearly gone now, only the rain remained. The rain reflected the lights of downtown as it sluiced down rooftops and the sides of buildings and ran in gutters toward drainage ditches.

"What about the others?" I asked.

"What others?"

"You don't know of any other murders that happened recently?" She shook her head. I wasn't sure I believed her.

"The boy who sold you the file out on the beach," I said. "Freddy."

"He's dead?"

"You didn't know?"

"No," she said. "I've been locked up in a room. How would I—I can't believe he's dead. He was such a sweet kid. He was just trying to help me. Who would kill him?"

"You tell me," I said. "Who would beat him to death?"

"He was beaten to death?" she asked, her voice breaking.

She began to sniffle a little, and I looked over to see a tear rolling down her cheek.

I still couldn't be sure if she were faking or not, so I decided to hit her with the death of her friend and see what happened.

"Lauren," I said. "Margie's dead too."

"No," she said. "Oh God, no."

"Beaten to death just like Freddy."

She began to cry harder. She seemed genuinely upset, but I still couldn't be sure. After all, she had been convincing when she told me she'd love me for the rest of her life, too.

"Lauren, what's going on?" I asked. "What are you involved in? It can't just be one of your extramarital indiscretions."

Her head was bowed forward, her face in her hands, little moans escaping periodically.

I pulled up in front of her house on Beach Drive overlooking the bay and parked next to the curb. The rain was only a light drizzle now, more mist than anything else, and the land and water, even the houses and cars, seemed clean and fresh.

"Let me help you," I said. "I can—"

"You're the last person who could help me," she said, opening her door. "All you can do is make things worse. Please, if you ever loved me, stay away from me."

Chapter 19

Too wound up after dropping Lauren off to even think about sleeping, I bought a bottle of Cobbs Creek and drove to the Dixie Sherman.

When Jan Christie opened the door of the small wooden lookout shack on the roof and saw me standing there agitated and holding a brown paper bag, she shook her head.

"Not tonight, soldier," she said. "We got a live one."

One of nearly ninety volunteers known as spotters, Jan spent several hours each night watching the sky for enemy aircraft. Her station was a small wooden enclosure on top of the Dixie Sherman. Like the other volunteers, she had been trained to identify aircraft—both ours and theirs—by sight and sound.

I wasn't sure if the "live one" she had tonight was one of theirs or one of ours.

The flyers of Tyndall Field were bad about buzzing the beaches and bridges, and our spotters spent most of their time "spotting" them instead of the Japs or Germans. Though the base had issued explicit orders that no planes were to be flown beneath 1,000 feet and north of Highway 98, there was still the occasional pilot who had to test his wings.

"I brought your favorite," I said, holding up the whiskey.

"Every time she's close enough to get her poison in you," she said, "you show up here wantin' me to cut the wound open and suck out the venom."

Not nearly as beautiful or regal as Lauren, there was something about Jan that made me think of her. It was in her attitude, her posture, the hunger beneath her plaid skirt and white blouse. She was right. I only used her, treating her the way Lauren had treated me, and finding temporary relief. Very temporary. And not just because I was so limited in what I could do. The next morning I would always feel far worse than Lauren ever made me feel, my self-inflicted sickness and inexcusable cruelty toward a girl whose only sin was letting me, making me hate myself more even than Lauren.

"Can I just sit here and drink?" I asked.

Before she could answer, her radio sounded and she stepped back inside her station.

Folding up my raincoat, I spread it out on the top of two wet wooden steps, sat down, and leaned on the door she had just closed. Holding the bottle between my legs, I broke the seal and unscrewed the cap with my hand. Dropping the cap and pushing back the paper bag, I turned up the bottle and took a long swig, letting the alcohol tingle my mouth and burn my throat.

Through the thin wooden door, I could hear the details of the situation they were dealing with. A flyer from Tyndall Field had already zoomed down beneath the Hathaway Bridge when it was open for boat traffic, and now that it was closed again, looked to be planning to fly beneath its span with vehicles on top of it.

"Guy's tryin' to kill himself," I said.

She didn't answer.

"Must've fallen for the wrong woman."

I took a few more pulls on the bottle and thought about what I was doing. I couldn't blame Lauren's power over me or Jan's weakness against me. I alone was responsible for the damage I was doing. I had become a carrier and was infecting her. I had to stop.

Standing up slowly, I placed the bottle down on the step I had been sitting on and walked away. When I reached the exit door, I told her I was sorry and that I wouldn't be back, but I wasn't sure she heard it.

When the elevator door opened in the lobby, I saw Ray standing there. He held up his hands in a defensive gesture.

"Don't hit me," he said. "Don't hit me."

I smiled. "Who knew Ray Parker had a sense of humor?" I said. "What are you doing here?"

"Meeting with Harry Lewis," he said.

"You two got a room?" I said.

"Don't judge, Jimmy," he said. "We might just turn out to be very happy together."

"Again with the humor," I said. "What gives?"

"Good day in court," he said.

I nodded.

"Any progress on finding Mrs. Lewis?"

I nodded again. "She's home."

His eyebrows shot up and he gave me a small nod.

"Impressive," he said. "You must have had a hell of a teacher. Where was she?"

"Sanatorium on Eleventh Street," I said. "Run by a quack named Rainer."

"Good work. As far as meeting with Harry," he said, "he thinks Frank Howell is playing dirty and may even be using his wife to do it."

"Lauren?"

"Don't jump to any conclusions," he said. "Wouldn't be the first time a husband was wrong about his wife."

I thought about what he had said and how Lauren had been acting.

"Whatta you think?" he asked.

"That Harry doesn't know his wife," I said. "She might cheat on him, but she'd never betray him."

"You headed home?" he asked.

I nodded.

"I'll swing by after I talk with Lewis," he said. "Let's see if we can't find a handle on this thing."

Chapter 20

When I got out of my car in front of the Cove Hotel and started toward my room, Pete and Butch stepped out of the shadows of a large shrub and walked toward me.

"Arms up," Butch said. "Well, arm."

I did as he said.

He walked up to me cautiously and patted me down, hitting me hard with his large hands.

"Where is it?" Butch asked.

"Where's what?"

It had stopped raining, but the air was still heavy with moisture, and the raindrop-covered surfaces all around us glistened in the lamp-lights.

Pete said, "Where have you been, Jimmy?"

"Where's what?" I asked.

"The piece you used," Butch said.

"For what?"

"Where you been, Jimmy?" Pete asked again.

"Around," I said. "Why?"

"It's awfully late," he said.

"It is," I said. "What are you boys doing up?"

"About to take you down, smart guy," Butch said.

"For what?"

"Come on, Jimmy," Pete said. "You gotta level with us. Why're you acting like this?"

"'Cause I don't trust your new partner," I said. "I haven't done anything, but he won't believe that. He's gonna keep on until he nails me for something and he doesn't care what or if I even did it."

"Nobody's looking to—"

"Why'd you kill him?" Butch asked.

"See?" I said to Pete, then turning to Butch, "Who?"

"Don't give me that," he said. "You know good and goddam well who."

I assumed he was talking about Mountain, but I wasn't about to say it. I wondered how they had tied me to his death so quickly. The night nurse? Did they have Clip? Would they go after Lauren?

"Pete," I said. "You gotta help me out here. At least tell me who I'm being framed for killing."

"Let's take a ride," he said.

"Do I have a choice?" I asked.

"No," Butch said.

"Come on, Jimmy," Pete said. "It's me. Don't make us your enemies. You know I'll help you out no matter what you've done."

He actually thought I might have done it, too.

"I think you mean *if* I've done anything," I said.

"*If* you took him out," he said, "you did us a favor, and we'll look out for you. Just don't play us for saps. That's all I'm saying."

The little gray gunsel the big guy had called Cab had been killed like the others. He had been beaten to death. He was sitting at the base of an oak tree in an empty lot just a few blocks from Rainer's sanatorium, his upper body slumped forward. His hat was missing and his wet hair hung down in front. The closest house was half a mile away.

"You think I did this?" I asked.

"You'll do just fine for it," Butch said.

"And you thought I was being paranoid," I said to Pete.

"He didn't mean it, Jimmy," he said. "Just tell us you didn't do it. Tell us where you were."

As Butch stared at the body, he rubbed his boxer's nose with his index finger.

The ground was soft and damp, wet blades of grass and bits of sand clinging to our shoes. Raindrops falling from oak leaves hit the earth with a dull thud and the nearby street with a wet slap.

"Why don't you two tell me a few things first," I said. "How did I get the drop on him? He's obviously a guy who carries a gun."

"Maybe you had a gun of your own," Butch said.

"Okay, so I've got a gun," I said. "I get the drop on him, take his gun, then—what?"

They had both reacted to something I said, their faces twitching before quickly recovering.

Pete reached down and pulled open Cab's soggy coat to reveal the butt of his gun still snugly in his shoulder holster.

"You just said that part about taking his gun 'cause you knew his gun was still holstered under his coat," Butch said.

I laughed and shook my head. "Hear that Pete? Things change that much since I left the force? It's not find who did it, but find someone you can pin it on."

"It ain't like that, Jimmy," Pete said. "I ain't gonna let anybody set you up for something you didn't do. Go ahead with what you were saying."

"So I've got a gun on him and his is in his coat," I said. "And since I can't hold a gun on him with one arm and hit him with another, he's kind enough to let me put my gun up, then begin to beat him to death with my left hand—all the while not fighting back or taking out his gun to convince me to stop hitting him."

Pete looked at Butch.

"How'd you know he had a gun?"

"His kind always do," I said.

He didn't say anything.

Butch pulled out a pack of Fleetwoods, tapped one out, put it in his mouth, and returned the pack to his coat pocket. He then tried to light it with a match, cupping his hands around the flickering flame. It took him a while, but he stuck with it and finally got it lit.

"The other thing that would bother me, this were my case," I said, "is why."

"Why what?" Butch asked.

"Why this guy?" I said. "What's my motive?"

"I'm sure it has something to do with a case you're working," Butch said.

"Butch," Pete said. "Come on. He's right. He didn't do this."

"If he didn't, he knows who did," he said.

I thought about Clip. Why didn't he just shoot him? I had never known him to beat a man to death when he had a perfectly good gun in his hand.

"Come on, Jimmy, I'll give you a ride home."

I turned to see Ray walking up behind us.

"He ain't goin' anywhere," Butch said. "We're just getting started."

"Hey Ray," Pete said.

"Pete," Ray said.

Everyone respected Ray. Even the cops.

"Who the hell you think you are?" Butch asked.

Well, the smart cops. Ray was not just another PI, but a legend—both as a cop and as a Pinkerton.

"Ask your boss," Ray said. "He and the DA will be here any minute."

"Sorry, Ray," Pete said. "He's new."

"Yeah?" Ray said. "What's your excuse?"

Ray turned and started walking away, and I followed.

Butch came up behind Ray. "Who the fuck do you think you are?" he said.

Ray kept walking.

"You hungry?" he said to me.

"I'm talking to you, asshole," Butch said, but Ray kept walking as if he weren't.

Butch made a few more comments before finally shoving Ray in the back with both his big hands. Ray didn't go forward far, which let me know he had been expecting it. He spun around and hit the big cop with a right hook that landed squarely on his left cheek, jerking his head around. He then snapped out a couple of hard left jabs and finished with a straight overhand right that put the large man on the ground. He turned as if nothing had happened and we continued walking toward his car.

Chapter 21

"Thanks," I said.

Ray didn't say anything.

"Butch's gonna retaliate," I said. "And he's not the kind that'll come at you from the front."

He nodded. "I'll try not to live in constant fear."

I smiled.

We rode along in silence for a few moments. The rain had moved out, but the world was still wet, a million tiny raindrops refracting Ray's headlights in the darkness.

"How'd you know where to find me?" I asked.

"Got a call from a friend of ours at the station," he said.

"Thanks for coming."

"Don't mention it, partner," he said.

That hurt. I hadn't been acting like a partner to him.

"Would you mind taking Eleventh Street?" I asked. "There's something I want to see."

"Sure," he said.

He cut over on one of the side streets, which enabled me to see both the front and the back of Rainer's sanatorium. It was dark and quiet. No disturbance. No cops. No nothing. Maybe they weren't going to call the police. Maybe they didn't want them involved any more than we did. If so, Rainer was far more crooked and Lauren in far more danger than I realized.

"You gonna tell me what's going on?" Ray asked.

I did. Most of it, anyway. I had been feeling guilty for keeping so much from him and he deserved to know—especially when his partner's picture was spending time on the front page of the paper under headlines that included the words "questioned in connection with a homicide investigation."

"How can I help?" he asked.

No rebuke. No reprimand. No Lauren lecture. Just the offer of assistance.

"I'm not sure," I said.

"What's your next move?"

"I'm not sure," I said again.

"Any idea who's behind the murders?"

I shook my head, though it was too dark for him to see it. "None," I said. "I was thinking maybe Rainer's men when I thought they were looking for Lauren, but he already had her—and that wouldn't explain who killed Cab."

"You don't think Clipper killed Cab?"

"You could swing by Shine Town and we could ask him."

Located in the easternmost section of St. Andrews and originally known as East End, Shine Town was the Negro community named after a big moonshiner named Shine who moved in after the mill closed and made and sold rum. Before him, back when it was East End, a man named Thompson ran a saw mill. Lumber from the head of East Bay was floated down to the head of Massalina Bayou, and the mill workers lived in homes built by the mill owner known as the quarters.

Clip lived in a small shack with a bunch of other Negroes. I didn't think all of them were part of his family, but I wasn't sure.

I banged on the sagging wooden door and waited. When it opened, I was staring down the serious end of a double-barrel shotgun, the only thing beside it I could see was the whites of one wide eye.

"Name's Jimmy Riley," I said. "I'm a friend of Clip's. He in?"

"Put your popgun down, Pookie," Clip said from somewhere in the small dark structure. "Cracker owes me money. Don't shoot him 'fore I collect."

The shotgun was lowered and I took a few steps back into the muddy front yard. When I looked back at Ray who was sitting in the car, he shook his head. In a moment, a shirtless Clipper Jones joined me.

"Good way to git your ass shot," he said. "Be a shame to lose that other arm."

"If you had a phone, I'd call first," I said.

"If you paid me better, I'd have a phone."

"That's why I'm here," I said. "We're gonna give you a bonus for what you did to the little gray man."

He looked confused.

I waited.

"You mean what I'll do to him when I find him?" he asked.

"I thought you had."

He shook his head.

"Somebody did."

"Who?" he said. "Who the cracker that took money out my pocket and how much I git, I take *him* out?"

"So if it wasn't Clipper or Rainer's goons," Ray said, "who was it?"

We were back in his car nearing downtown.

"No idea."

"You don't think the girl could have—

"No," I said. "No way."

"Okay, partner," he said. "I just thought somebody should ask."

"What about her husband?"

"Harry?"

"Or someone he hired."

"He hired me."

"And you have no idea what Mrs. Lewis is hiding?" he asked.

I shook my head. "No," I said, "but it probably involves a man her husband doesn't know about."

He pulled up in front of the Cove Hotel and parked at the curb but didn't kill his engine.

"You gonna be okay?" he asked.

I nodded, which in the streetlamp he could see.

"What'd Lewis say?" I asked.

"That Howell is bent," he said, "and we'd be far better off with him as mayor. Can't just hire us. Has to make political speeches first. Wants us to find out what Howell is up to, if he's using someone close to Harry."

"You tell him it wasn't his wife?" I asked.

He shook his head. "Didn't come up."

"You take the job?"

He nodded. "Told him I'd work it in when I wasn't in court, helping you, working other cases, or running our agency."

"And what'll you do on the weekends?" I asked. "Wipe out the Japs and Germans?"

Chapter 22

When I walked into the office the next morning, July frowned at me, and I wondered if she already knew about last night.

"I'm doing the best I can," I said.

"What are you talking about?" she asked.

"Why are you frowning at me?"

She handed me a small slip of paper. "Lauren Lewis called," she said, her frown deepening.

A small flock of butterflies fluttered around my stomach, and I was unable to suppress a certain twitching of my lips.

I had always thought that if I could have her just one more time, I could get her out of my system. *If I could have her and be the one to leave* . . . I couldn't have her now, but if she wanted me and I could reject her, then maybe I could be free of her.

"I thought you were going to stay away from her?"

"I am," I said.

"Then why is she calling you?"

I shrugged. "I don't know. What'd she say?"

I looked at the small slip of paper, resisting the urge to rub my finger over her name.

"I'm not sure I can remember," she said with a wry smile. "In fact, I may have forgotten to write her number down."

She snatched the paper from my grasp and looked at it.

"I sure did," she said. "How could I be so stupid? Well, I am just a part-time secretary. It's not like anyone around here trusts me enough to do something important."

At first I thought it was just because she wanted to spend more time with Ray, but I had increasingly become convinced that July really wanted to be a detective.

She then wadded up the paper into a little ball and tossed it into the small trash can behind her.

"Rations," I said. "The war. Ring any bells? I don't think you're supposed to be wasting paper."

"You're just sore you don't have the number."

"Yeah, that's it," I said, heading toward my office. "It's not like I could still remember it or find it in the directory."

In my office, I snatched up the receiver, punched in the number, and sat down.

After two impossibly long rings, a man's voice answered.

I hesitated a minute, then said in my most professional tone, "Lauren Lewis, please."

"Who?"

"Lauren Lewis."

"Wrong number."

I repeated the number I had dialed.

"Right number," he said. "Wrong person."

"How long have you had this number?"

"About six months. Any other personal information I can give you, pal?"

"Sorry," I said and hung up.

Everything changes, I thought. *Everything has changed.*

I walked around my desk and collapsed into my chair.

When Ray walked in a few minutes later, he sat down in one of the client chairs across from me without saying a word.

We sat that way for a long time, and there was far more solace in it than had we been talking.

Our building was as quiet as a library, which is what Ray said my office resembled more than anything else. Glancing around the room at all the used books, I thought he just might be right. Even July, who usually had the small radio on her desk playing as she worked, was silent.

Out on Harrison, the morning traffic moved slowly and quietly. The little shops lining it were doing a steady business, but at a leisurely pace, as if the only people shopping, the retired and the rich, had nothing to do in the world but browse and buy.

"Still no word about the big guy Clipper shot at Rainer's," Ray said. "Cops don't know anything about it."

"He's covering it up," I said. "Means he's got a lot to hide."

He nodded.

"Election's soon," he said. "Whatever's going on is tied to that."

I nodded.

"It's not over," he said.

"I know."

"We've had this conversation, but I didn't like your answer," he said. "Would you let me handle it for you?"

"I can't," I said.

He nodded.

"But thanks," I said.

He stood. "If there's anything I can do to help," he said, "let me know. I'm headed to court."

Without waiting for my response, he turned and walked out, pausing to speak to July in the reception area.

A call came in, and July answered it. I could tell by her voice it was Lauren. "For you," she yelled.

Chapter 23

I picked up the receiver, wishing my door was closed.

"Did you get my message?" she asked.

"Yeah," I said, "but I thought you said all you had to say last night."

"Oh."

We were both silent an awkward moment and I started to say something, but didn't want to make this any easier on her. It was as if we hadn't seen each other since our affair ended.

"I'm sorry for the way I acted last night," she said. "I was upset and undone by everything. And it's always confusing for me to be around you."

"You know, I don't think July wrote down a number for you," I said.

"She doesn't like me."

"Is it the same?"

"No, actually," she said. "I gave her the new number, but . . ."

"What is it?" I asked.

After she gave it to me, she said, "I was wondering . . ."

"Yeah?"

"If we might have lunch," she said slowly, "perhaps tomorrow."

I hesitated before answering. "Actually, I'm in the middle of a big case right now. Could we make it for later in the week?"

"Oh, ah, sure," she said as if she weren't.

"Thursday?"

"Okay."

"Carson's? Mattie's? Where?" I asked.

"How about the Cove?" she asked.

That would put us having lunch just a few feet away from my room. *Is that what she intended?*

"Do you get tired of eating there?" she added.

"No," I said. "The Cove is fine."

"Thanks for being willing to meet me," she said.

"Oh, I eat lunch everyday," I said. "It's no bother."

I sat there, the sound of my pounding heart in my head, moist palm gripping the receiver.

Finally, I slammed it down, then picked it up again and punched in the number she had just given me.

"Lauren," I said when she answered. "Things have changed."

She was quiet for a long moment before softly saying, "Yeah?"

"Yeah," I said. "Tomorrow will be fine."

"Thank you, Jimmy."

Hearing her say my name brought back the stirring inside I'd felt before. I hadn't thought it was possible, but maybe it was. Was it just in my mind or was something happening? Perhaps we would go to my room tomorrow after lunch and find out.

Long after she had hung up, I sat there holding the phone to my ear, straining to remember how my name had sounded in her mouth. Knowing all the while that she was going to be the end of me, but unable to care.

"What'd that phone ever do to you?" July asked.

I turned to look at her, slowly coming out of my trance. Realizing I still clutched the receiver in my hand, I gently replaced it in the cradle.

"Huh?"

"Someone to see you," she said.

I raised my eyebrows.

"A guy," she said. "Kinda handsome."

"Send him in."

She did.

Cliff Walton, Harry Lewis's head of security, walked in and sat down across from me.

Without preamble, he withdrew an envelope from his inside coat pocket and handed it to me. I took it. It felt heavy, like corruption. I handed it back to him.

"Mr. Lewis is very pleased with your work on the safe return of his wife," he said. "He wishes to thank you."

"Tell him he's welcome," I said.

"He wishes to pay you."

"Just give me a little information and we'll call it squared."

He put the envelope back in his pocket, probably planning to keep it for himself. "Information concerning what exactly?"

"The whole thing," I said. "Mrs. Lewis, the election, everything."

"What do you wish to know?"

"I wish to know what the hell is going on," I said.

"I don't follow."

"Start with Mrs. Lewis," I said. "What's she mixed up in?"

"You know more about it than I do," he said.

"If you weren't gonna tell me anything you should have just said so."

"I don't know anything to tell."

"Okay," I said. "Play it that way, but there's a string of dead bodies lined up after the lady, and I ain't takin' the fall for them."

"Are you sure they're lined up after the lady?" he said. "I understood from the police that they were left behind everywhere you'd been."

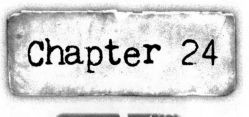

Chapter 24

I was sitting at a table near the front trying not to look up too anxiously every time the door opened. Hoping to arrive after her, I had come a full ten minutes late, something that took restraint, but I had still managed to arrive well ahead of her.

I could feel myself beginning to break apart inside. I did okay when I was with her for the most part, but when we weren't together I felt weak with wanting her, my mind unable to fight off the taunts and questions, the accusations, the depression.

I glanced around the room, attempting to settle myself, but everywhere I looked I was reminded of her, of our many times together here. We would often meet here for lunch, say our public goodbyes, then walk separately to my room.

Who was she doing that with now? And where? How many other men had there been since me? How many of them thought of her as *theirs*? How many of them had a regular meeting place and cooks and waiters and maids who unwittingly became co-conspirators in their duplicity?

Business men, tourists, and men on leave kept the door opening, my head bobbing. They came in small groups, usually no more than four, but never alone.

I thought about how many meals I ate alone—not because I had to, but because if I couldn't be with her it really didn't matter.

I could feel the muscles in my neck and shoulders tensing as anger rose from the pit of me up through them, and then . . .

The scent of Paris and the gentle touch of an elegant hand on my arm.

I turned to see her standing there behind me in a short, straight black dress and mules, the burns on her bare arms and legs more visible than I had ever seen them in public.

I stood.

Unable to avert my eyes from her body, unsuccessful at suppressing my attraction in spite of my best efforts—after all she had left me, lied to me repeatedly, put me and my friends in danger—desire gripped me like fear. I was drunk with it. It mixed with my rage and resentment and I felt clumsy and sluggish as I stumbled self-consciously to pull out her chair.

"I've missed this," she said when we were seated across from one another at the table. "I didn't realize just how much until now."

I nodded, looking around the room and then out the window.

The molten gold glow of the midday sun covering the water made the bay shine and sparkle, its reflection forming a haze that surrounded a small sailboat in the distance as if a poorly developed picture on overexposed film.

"Well," our waitress said as she reached the table, "there's two faces I haven't seen together in a while."

"Too long," Lauren said.

After telling us what we wanted, the waitress went off to brighten someone else's day, and we were alone again.

"Thanks again for coming," she said. "After the way I've acted lately, I wouldn't have blamed you if you didn't."

I left that alone and we made awkward small talk until our food came. We ate in silence, and though I was happy just to be with her, I was experiencing conflicting emotions, and I couldn't help but feel like a fool.

As we finished eating, I said, "Are you ready to tell me what's going on?"

"It's over," she said. "Thanks to you. I'm free of that awful sanatorium and I'm not going back."

"Why were you there?"

"Just all the pressure of public life and the campaign," she said. "I needed a little break, but the timing was bad."

"Lauren," I said. "That's not even halfway convincing."

She didn't say anything.

"What does Rainer have on you? Or Harry? What did you pay Freddy for?"

"That was nothing," she said. "Unrelated to anything else."

"You're lying."

"You're trying to make something where there is nothing," she said. "Nothing's going on."

"All the dead bodies contradict you," I said.

"I'm very sorry about them, but I didn't have anything to do with them, don't know anything about them."

"If you were just going to continue to lie to me, why ask to see me at all?"

"I didn't want things between us to end the way they did."

She still wants us to have something we never will—a good ending.

"I asked you here," she continued, "to apologize and—"

"You already did that," I said.

"And to ask you to help Harry."

"Help Harry?"

"I know he's going to ask you to protect him," she continued. "I just didn't want anything I had done to stop you from—"

"Nothing you've done would stop me from anything," I said. "I wouldn't lose a job for revenge."

"If you knew how little you had to revenge . . ."

I didn't say anything and we fell silent a moment.

"Harry's a good man and he'll make a great mayor, but there are—"

"Don't appeal to me on politics," I said. "I'm sure mine and Harry's aren't the same."

"You'd be surprised," she said. "You should talk to him."

I nodded. "You're right," I said. "I should. We could compare wounds and war stories."

"You don't have to be cruel," she said. "Everything's not as it seems."

I considered her. "You don't have to tell me that."

She looked down into her empty glass.

"Was that all you wanted to see me about?" I asked. "Helping Harry?"

She started to say something, hesitated, then swallowed hard and nodded.

"Well, we may or may not take the job," I said. "It's really up to Ray, but you don't have to worry about anything you've done stopping me from taking money from a rich politician. And, as you already know, I have no problem taking anything that belongs to Harry."

Chapter 25

When I got back to the office, July was frantic.

"Where the hell have you been?" she asked.

"What is it?"

"Ray," she said. "He's been arrested."

"For what?" I asked. "By who?"

"I don't know," she said. "Some big mean guy I didn't recognize. He came here about an hour ago. Ray had just gotten back from the courthouse. He had just enough time to return a few calls and eat a sandwich and this guy comes in with a gun, flashes his badge, tells him he's under arrest, cuffs him, and takes him out."

I thought about it.

"Was the guy older, dark complexion, nose been broken, looked like a fighter?"

She was nodding before I finished. "Who is he?"

"Name's Butch," I said. "He's Pete's new partner. Was he alone?"

She nodded. "I called the station, but he hasn't been booked yet."

"That's because he's not going to be," I said. "He's not really being arrested. Butch is trying to square something with him. It's personal."

"What's he gonna do?"

I shrugged. "Beat him up or kill him," I said.

"What're you gonna do?"

"I have no idea."

"Hi ya, Jimmy," Pete said.

"Where's your partner, Pete?" I asked.

He was having a late lunch at Carson's, his plate piled high with fried seafood. He was sitting alone and had just gotten his food when I walked up.

"What?" he asked, his fork full of fish and cheese grits poised in front of his mouth.

"Where's Butch?"

He shrugged to give himself time to chew and swallow. "No idea," he said, talking around the food still in his mouth. "He's off today. Why?"

"He just arrested Ray."

"For what?"

"Revenge," I said.

"He's got to have a charge, Jimmy," he said. "You know—"

"Not if he's not taking him to jail."

His eyes widened and he dropped his fork on his plate, knocking a hush puppy on the table. Jumping up, he all but ran out to his car. I followed him.

Leaving his door open, Pete sat in the driver's side, feet on the ground, radio in hand. I stood over him, my left hand gripping the top of his door.

Radioing headquarters, he quickly confirmed that Butch had not taken Ray there. He then asked the dispatcher to radio Butch and have him contact his partner immediately. When he signed off, he tried repeatedly to reach Butch. There was no response.

"Where would he take him?" I asked.

He looked up at me, helplessness in his eyes. "I have no idea. He's new. We just—"

"Think, Pete," I said. "For your partner as much as Ray. This could end his career or worse. Where would he take him?"

Pete looked up and narrowed his eyes, his forehead wrinkling, bright red lines against his pale skin.

"It'd have to be somewhere secluded," I said. "Where does he live?"

"Boarding house in Lynn Haven," he said.

"What does he do?" I asked. "Any hobbies? Does he hunt? Fish? What?"

My voice was loud and intense, and several customers entering and exiting Carson's stopped to look, catching Pete's eye to make sure everything was okay, continuing after he nodded to them.

"I just don't know, Jimmy. I'd tell you if I did. You know that."

"You wanna go ahead and arrest me now?" I said.

"What?" he asked, his voice high and surprised. "For what?"

"Whatever he does to Ray I'm gonna square," I said.

"You ain't a cop, Jimmy."

"Neither is he," I said. "He's off the book on this one, Pete, and you know it."

"Wait," Pete said suddenly, standing up only to sit back down. "Get in," he added, and slammed his door.

Less than two weeks ago, Butch had been part of a group of cops who discovered and busted up a moonshine still in the pinewoods near Sandy Creek. Since moonshine had soared from eight to fifty dollars for a five-gallon jug, stills had sprouted up all over the Panhandle. Even employees of Wainwright Shipyard with good jobs were quitting to become ridge runners instead. Shootings, stabbings, and instances of lead poisoning had dramatically increased.

We raced down Highway 22 toward Wewahitchka, taking a left on Sandy Creek Road, then another left on a twin path logging trail.

"How we gonna play this, Pete?" I asked.

"Just like old times," he said. "We're gonna stop him all peaceful-like if we can."

"And if we can't?" I asked.

"He's my partner, Jimmy," he said. "Let's try not to shoot him."

"That's totally up to him."

As we reached the small clearing that held the hand-operated pitcher pump connected to the shallow well, the various metal vats and buckets, the hoses and hardware, and what was left of the over-turned and smashed barrels, we saw Butch's car. It was parked at an angle that partially blocked our view.

I jumped out before Pete had fully stopped the car.

Pulling my gun out of my shoulder holster as I ran, I came around Butch's car to find Ray kneeling down in front of an open well, his hands cuffed behind him, Butch standing over him, his gun pointed at the back of Ray's head.

"Drop the gun," I said.

Without moving the gun, Butch turned slightly and looked at me, shaking his head as he did.

"How the hell did you find me?"

"Doesn't matter," I said. "Drop the gun."

He shook his head. "How good a shot are you with your left hand?" he asked.

"Be easier for me to show you than tell you," I said.

He smiled.

"I don't think you could hit me from there," he said.

"Fail to drop your gun, you'll find out."

I was beginning to wonder where Pete was until I saw him step out of the woods on the other side of Butch with his gun drawn.

"We got the drop on you, partner," he said. "Put your gun down now so nobody gets hurt."

Butch slowly turned to look at Pete, and I edged closer to him. He was right about my left-handed shooting skills—even after nearly a year of practice.

"How the hell can you call me partner?" Butch asked. "You're pointing a gun at me, and you brought the one-armed dick over there to—what? Take me out?"

"I'm doin' my best to help you, partner," Pete said. "Jimmy's here for his new partner and I'm here for mine. You don't want to do this. It's not too late. Just drop your weapon."

"Maybe you're right," Butch said. "I just can't let a civilian put his paws on me and not . . ."

"I know," Pete said. "But this isn't the way."

"I just wanted to scare him," Butch said. "I wasn't gonna really hurt him."

"I know," Pete said.

I didn't know it, and I doubted even Butch knew it, but if it got us out of this standoff, let him say it all he wanted.

Butch nodded, holstered his weapon, and reached down and uncuffed Ray. "No hard feelings," Butch said. "I'm glad my partner came along and kept me from doing something stupid."

If I doubted Butch was insane before, I didn't now. He was certifiable, which made him far more dangerous than if he were just mean. I'd be willing to bet that a call to Miami PD would get a story of an unstable cop who transferred out to a podunk department just ahead of a reprimand or termination or even an indictment.

"Let's all leave friendly like," Butch said. "Let bygones be by-gones, and if you don't want to do that, then just remember I still have my gun."

Butch backed up to give Ray plenty of room to stand.

"Everything jake there Raymond?" Butch said.

"Far from it," he said. "But we're done for today."

Butch nodded. "You calling a truce?"

Ray nodded. "A very temporary one," he said, took a quick step forward and popped Butch's scarred face with a hard overhand right.

It was a clean, well-delivered shot that didn't just knock Butch down, but out.

"Keep him away from me, Pete," Ray said. "Next time I'll kill him."

"I'll try," he said.

"Be a good idea to get him out of town," Ray said. "Early retirement or something."

"We'll take your car back to town, Pete," I said. "You can drive Butch back in his. I'll leave it for you at the station. And thanks for your help."

"Sure thing, Jimmy," he said. "And I'm very sorry for what happened, Ray."

"Thanks to you and Jimmy," Ray said, "it was what almost happened. I won't forget that Pete."

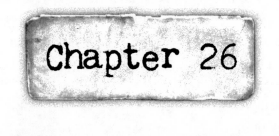

Chapter 26

The Lodge at Wakulla Springs was a popular recreational spot for servicemen, so I was surprised when the man who greeted Lauren at the room door wasn't in uniform.

I was following Lauren again.

I had a pocket full of ration coupons for food, but I had used my last one for gas. If Lauren was going to continue to lead me all over the Panhandle, I'd have to turn to bribery or the black market.

It was obvious she wasn't going to tell me what was really going on, but that didn't mean I wouldn't find out. All this had started with her coming to my office because she thought I was following her, and now I was. The irony wasn't lost on me.

One of the world's largest and deepest freshwater springs, Wakulla Springs hosts an abundance of wildlife, including alligators, turtles, and many species of birds. Its clear, cool waters, complex cave system, and surrounding forests make for recreation that's as beautiful as it is refreshing.

Located just south of Tallahassee, the springs have been of scientific interest since 1850 when Sarah Smith saw the bones of an ancient mastodon on the bottom. Over the past ninety years, scientists have identified the remains of several other extinct Ice Age mammals. But that wasn't why most people came to the springs. It was for swimming, boat rides, relaxation, and the observation of wildlife—mostly relaxation, to forget about the war, and the hopes of amorous activities.

Built in 1937 by railroad magnate Edward Ball, the Mediterranean Revival style Wakulla Springs Lodge has hand-wrought iron, marble, and hand-made ceramic imported tile. Its twenty-seven rooms are luxurious and spacious.

At the time, the lodge was managed by Newton Perry, a famous swim coach who brought Hollywood to the springs. Thanks to him the first Tarzan movie, featuring Olympic swimmer Johnny Weissmuller, was filmed here a couple of years ago.

Lauren was in a room with a man who looked nearly as old as Harry. Maybe that was the problem. I was too young for her—we were the same age.

I was sitting in the enormous lobby next to the massive fireplace reading the paper when I wasn't looking out the tall arched windows at the bathers enjoying the warm sun (it was warm for October even by Florida standards) on the beach, in the water, and on the dive platform. Beyond them, the Tarpon Club, the synchronized swim team of Florida State College for Women, was training.

The paper was old, but I didn't mind. I was using it for cover, and I had been too busy to read much of it lately anyway. At least it was full of good news for our side (the past several I had looked at were depressing—especially the one that announced that German forces were occupying Rome). In this one the allies were on a roll, and having recently captured Naples, we had now gained control of Corsica.

After nearly two hours, the man appeared on the stairs, walked through the lobby right past me, and continued into the dining room.

He ordered a cup of coffee, and I violated every rule in the Shamus Manual by walking over to make a little conversation with him.

"Morning," I said as I sat down at the table next to him.

"Hi ya, soldier," he said. "How you been?"

He was a friendly sort, his face and eyes showing his openness. He had dark wavy hair beginning to go gray, a fleshy face, and a dark complexion.

"Been better," I said.

He nodded toward my folded up right sleeve. "We appreciate what you boys are doing for us and the world."

"God bless America," I said.

"Amen," he said.

We were silent a moment, as the waitress brought his coffee and took my order for the same.

"If you'd ever like to talk," he said, "I'm a grand listener."

I detected a bit of an Irish lilt in his voice I hadn't heard before.

"Aren't you after being kind?" I said with a wee smile.

He gave me one of his own and said, "Tis true," his accent growing much heavier. "I'm altogether Irish. And wouldn't I be after missing my homeland terrible bad?"

"What brings you here?" I asked.

"Now isn't that a long story?" he said.

"I meant to Wakulla Springs."

"Just visiting for the day," he said. "Live nearby in Panama City."

"That pretty woman with you your wife?"

"Oh no," he said. "Nothing like that."

I raised my eyebrows and smiled at him appreciatively.

A broad smiled spread across his face and I wanted to stand up and knock it off.

"Alas, I walk this weary world alone," he said.

"She looks familiar," I said. "I could swear I've seen her somewhere before."

He didn't take the bait and I let it go.

When my coffee came, I told him I was going to take it outside and said my goodbyes. It was just in time, too. As I reached the back door, I could hear Lauren's heels clicking on the marble floor, crossing the lobby toward him.

From one of the large arched windows, I watched as she hugged him with more genuine affection than she had ever shown me, and turned to leave.

I ran around the outside of the lodge and was in my car when she walked out the front door, but to my surprise, she didn't leave. She tossed a few things in her car and walked around the side of the lodge and down to the water's edge in the back, where she captured the attention of a few of the young guys lying on the beach nearby.

I followed, giving her plenty of room. There wasn't much to hide behind except an occasional tree.

Having left her house this morning too early to finish fixing her hair, Lauren had on a do-rag covering her curls, which had surprised me. She usually took better care before meeting lovers. Was she just that anxious or was she breaking apart?

When she reached the edge of the spring, she knelt down, took off her do-rag, cupped water in her hand, and sprinkled it on her head. She was wearing a dress. It wasn't that hot. She looked insane. A few of the guys who had been eyeing her lasciviously were now laughing at her.

"You're getting your dress wet, lady," one of the guys said. "Why don't you take it off?"

She stood and began to unbutton her dress. Before she could get very far or I could get to her, her current lover came running through one of the back doors and down to her.

"You okay, dear?" he asked.

She didn't say anything, just looked up at him with a faraway stare.

"Come on," he said. "Let me drive you home. I'll come back and get my car later."

Following Lauren and the older Irish man back to her car, I wondered if maybe the strain of the campaign or her double life was getting to her. It would explain why she was acting so strangely. Was that really what Dr. Rainer was treating her for?

I felt a heaviness, a weight bearing down on me from above, and a pressure in my chest. It was horrible to see her this way. I tried to recall anything unusual she did when we were together—any erratic or irrational behavior that might point to mental illness, but couldn't come up with anything.

Maybe I was wrong. Maybe she was fine. She could have just been upset by something that happened with Old Irish. Did she feel rejected? Defiled? Was she attempting to wash her sin away with the clear cool waters of the spring?

Once the old guy had her tucked into the passenger side of her car and was walking around the back to the driver's side, I appeared next to him.

"Is she okay?" I asked.

"She will be," he said.

"What's wrong with her?" I asked. "She seems—"

"It's exhaustion," he said. "Stress. She just needs rest."

"Anything I can do?" I asked.

"You could say a prayer for her," he said.

"Anything else?" I asked. "I wouldn't know what to say."

Chapter 27

In startling contrast to the woman who I witnessed unraveling at Wakulla Springs, the Lauren Lewis attending the political debate between her husband and Frank Howell was enchanting and erudite. When she walked into the room with her short, straight gray skirt and its matching short jacket, everyone turned—many never quite able to turn away from her for the rest of the evening.

We were in the cafeteria of Bay High School. The crowd was good, and included all the local dignitaries and luminaries, the top officials from Tyndall Field, the naval section base, and Wainwright Shipyard, the governor, a senator, a congressman, Pete and Butch, Ann Everett, and Payton Rainer. Rainer sat in the center of the front row. July was near the middle of the room, and Clip was with a small group of Negroes in the back. They were both here to help me find out who was following Lauren.

Ray and I were standing on one side of the stage, Cliff Walton on the other. Harry and the rotund man he was running against were standing near the front center of the platform, each trying to upstage the other.

"Any closer to finding out what's going on?" Ray whispered.

I shook my head.

Harry and Howell were taking turns talking about how important the working man (and now woman) was to them, the local economy, and the war effort.

"You ever get to talk to Rainer again?" he asked.

I shook my head. "I was waiting to see if there was any heat from us liberating Lauren, then the few times I stopped by, he wasn't there—they let me look. I figured he had left the country."

"Maybe we can have a chat with him after this is over," he said.

"You really think this thing's ever going to end?" I said. "You're more of an optimist than I thought."

He smiled. "You think Butch'll try to shoot me tonight?"

"He might right here in front of everyone," I said. "He ain't right. Cops any closer to finding out who killed Freddy, Margie, or Cab?"

"We're about to find out," he said, nodding toward the crowd.

I looked in the direction of his nod to see Pete making his way from his seat over toward us.

"Jimmy," he whispered, as he came up behind us. "Ray."

"Pete," I said.

Ray didn't speak.

"What's new?" Pete said.

"Not much," I said.

"Butch kidnapped or killed anyone lately?" Ray asked.

"Not today."

We were all quiet a moment. Pete was nervous and it showed. He knew as well as I did that it was just a matter of time until Butch did something stupid, and if he did it to Ray he was going to get killed.

"Any headway on who killed the kid, Margie, or Cab?" Pete said.

"You're asking *me*?"

"Yeah."

"No," I said. "You?"

"Not much," he said. "But I gotta do something with all these bodies. My captain's gettin' sore as hell."

I nodded.

Harry stood still as he spoke to the increasingly restless audience, but Howell moved about the stage on his toes in a way that reminded me of a cartoon I'd seen of a dancing hippopotamus in a tutu.

"Whoever did it is good," he said. "We got none of the normal eyewitnesses and not a single clue—except your card."

Ray raised his eyebrows as he looked over at me. I hadn't told him about my business card being found inside Margie.

"A pro?" I asked.

"Maybe," he said.

"Do you know where Butch was during the time of the murders?" Ray asked.

"It's not Butch," Pete said, but he didn't sound very confident.

We were quiet a moment, which forced us to hear Howell tell how he had far more integrity and had worked harder his whole life than the soft, money-loving banker, Lewis.

"You guys working for Howell or Lewis?" Pete asked.

"Yeah," I said, nodding.

"Come on, Jimmy," he said. "Just 'cause you don't work for the good guys anymore don't meant you have to work against us."

"I just don't want to do anything to help your partner frame me," I said. "Or shoot Ray."

"You mean die tryin' to shoot Ray," Ray said.

"Okay," Pete said. "Have it your way. Just answer one question for me. I know you're working for Lewis and that eager young wife of his. I just want to know if you were when all those people were killed."

He had been my partner. I had been willing to die for him the way I now was for Ray. And I wanted to turn around and use all the strength I had to beat his face in until it was unrecognizable. Somehow I found the restraint I needed to refrain, and he eased back over and took his seat beside his new partner, who was glaring in our direction.

"You think we acted like that when we were still part of the good guys?" Ray asked.

"I didn't," I said. "I'm sure you were far worse."

He smiled.

Eventually, the debate ended. There wasn't a clear winner among the candidates, but everyone in the audience was a loser. Frank Howell made his way down our side of the platform to greet his supporters, but Harry lingered on stage. He was staring at Rainer who was obviously trying to communicate something with his expression. His head was lowered, his eyebrows arched, and he looked from Lewis to Lauren and pointed to his watch.

I started to move toward Rainer, but stopped when Harry began to speak.

"Folks," Harry yelled over the noisy crowd. "Folks. Could I have your attention for a moment. I'm sorry, but there's something I need to say."

The crowd quieted down. Rainer was nodding at Harry. Lauren, who was shaking her head, looked over at me, her expression one of fear and helplessness. Howell, who was near me, looked over and arched his eyebrows.

Standing so close to him, I saw again how deep and abundant the acne scars on his face were and thought that he was benefitted by being on stage—too far away for potential voters to see just how unattractive a man he really was.

"I was going to wait to do this, but I feel I must say something tonight," he said. "I'm seriously considering dropping out of the race for mayor of this great city. If I do, it will be for purely personal reasons. I'd like nothing more than to get the opportunity to serve all of you fine folks, but sometimes . . . well, we don't always get what we want. I'll make my final decision in a couple of days and make an announcement then. For now, please keep me and my family in your prayers."

"Well," Howell said, his smile expanding his fat face even farther. "My, my." Winking at me, he added, "Wonder what kind of personal issues he has."

He then pranced away—well, as much as a slightly effeminate, elephantine middle-aged man can.

I looked for Rainer again, but he was gone.

"Did you know anything about this?" I asked Ray.

He shook his head.

"Wonder what's going on?" I asked.

"Let's see if we can't act like detectives and find out."

Chapter 28

"Take him around back and wait there," Walt said. "I'll get the car and pull around."

Ray and I began to escort Harry away from the crowd, which was still demanding an explanation from him.

"And see if you can find Mrs. Lewis," he added.

"I'll look for her," Ray said. "You take him."

Without waiting for a response, he disappeared into the crowd, and I grabbed Harry's right arm and ushered him toward the rear of the building.

We walked down a series of short, mostly dark hallways and wound up in a small storage room with a back door exit.

"We'll wait in here until Walt comes around with the car," I said.

He didn't say anything, only continued to look lost, as if he were the one who was in shock instead of the one who had delivered it.

"You okay?" I asked.

"I have all the money I'll ever need," he said, his voice small. He still had the unfocused stare of the desperate. "I just wanted to do something meaningful with my life. Help the people of the city that's been so good to me and my family. All I ever wanted to do was serve the public."

"Why are you considering pulling out of the race?" I asked.

He didn't look at me, didn't acknowledge my presence in any way.

"I would've made a great mayor," he said. "Lot of money and people flowing into our little town right now. Lot of corruption. We need someone who can't be bought, who'll stand up to those who would try to destroy our way of life. I could have done that. I—"

"Harry," I said, my voice loud and urgent.

He looked at me.

"What the hell's going on?" I asked. "Why are you dropping out of the race?"

"It's very personal," he said. "I don't want to, but I have to. They wanted me to drop out tonight, but I just couldn't. I keep hoping a miracle will happen."

"Who's they?" I asked. "Who's doing this to you?"

He didn't say anything, just shook his head.

The storage room was damp, and I could hear water dripping in an unseen corner. Pungent and difficult to breathe, it smelled of mildew and cleaning chemicals.

"Does it involve your wife?" I asked.

He sobered up instantly, turning his blue eyes on me with clarity and intensity. "My wife?" he asked. "What you are talking about?"

"Are they using your wife to get to you?" I asked.

"She has nothing to do with this," he said.

"Who killed Freddy Moats?" I asked.

"Who?"

"What does Rainer have on you?"

His eyes widened slightly, but he quickly recovered.

"Let us help you," I said. "We can make this go away. You just have to trust us. Isn't that why you hired us?"

"There's nothing you can do," he said. "Just pray for our city. Those who control it are going to take it down."

"Is Howell behind this?" I asked.

The rear door opened, and Walt and Ray were standing there.

"Come on, Mr. Lewis," Walt said. "Let's get you home."

"Where's Lauren?" I asked.

Both Walt and Lewis looked at me in surprise.

"I couldn't find her," Ray said. "She's gone. Somebody said they saw her walking."

"Probably walked home to clear her head," Lewis said.

"I'll go see if I can find her," I said. "See if you can get him to level with you. He's not dropping out of the race because he wants to."

Chapter 29

The lakeside park was cut out of a corner of pine and oak forest about a mile from downtown. It had a red brick entrance with a wrought-iron gate, a walking path, picnic pavilion, swings, and a merry-go-round for children.

The sliver of cloud-shrouded moon and smattering of stars against the black velvet sky did little to illuminate the dark night, and the streetlamps scattered throughout the park spilled only a small pool of light onto the ground directly beneath them.

Except for Lauren, the park appeared to be empty. Very few people would find it inviting on such a dark and foggy night. The playground equipment sat still and quiet, the only evidence children had been there recently, their tiny shoe prints in the sand around it.

Lauren, clutching her purse in her hands, walked along the path, her head down, her movements labored.

I scanned the park, my eyes moving across the wooden benches and swings, through the picnic tables on concrete pads and the grills a few feet away from them, past the pavilion, the public restrooms, the play area, and down to the cypress trees next to the black lake. At least one other person was here, watching from the woods or some other hidden vantage point, I knew it. I couldn't see him, but I could feel him.

"Nice night for a walk," Clip said, stepping out of the darkness to stand beside me.

We were beneath a large oak tree, hidden by a tall shrub near the entrance of the park. I had asked for his help after the debate, and he had been watching Lauren ever since, even while I was with Harry in the back of the school.

"She being followed?" I asked.

"You mean 'sides us?" he asked.

"Yeah."

He nodded.

"Any idea where he is?"

He shrugged. "Haven't seen him myself. July got a quick peek at him when he—"

"Where's July?"

He pulled one of Ray's Handie-Talkies up out of the darkness, extended the antenna to turn it on, and called for July.

The Gavlin Handie-Talkie units belonged to Ray. He had recovered them in a case he worked a year or so back and held onto them, thinking we might need them one day. I don't think Clip and July using them is what he had in mind.

"I'm here," July said. "There's someone following the little—" Clip depressed the button to speak so I wouldn't hear what she called Lauren. "—and I'm going in for a closer look at the guy."

I held out my hand for the unit.

"It was her idea," he said. "She had them in her car."

"July, this is Jimmy," I said. "Stay where you are. I repeat. Stay where you are."

"Jimmy?" she asked.

"Whoever he is, he's very good," I said. "Probably plenty dangerous, too. I want you to back away. Go get in your car and go home. We've got it from here."

"I ain't goin' anywhere, fella," she said.

"Does Ray know you have his radios?" I asked.

She didn't answer.

"Just stay where you are," I said. "I'll get back to you in a minute."

The lake was so dark it looked like an oil spill, its black surface shimmering like a Florida highway on an August afternoon, with the elongated reflections of the lights from the houses on the other side.

"How we gonna play this?" Clip asked.

"I'm open to suggestions," I said.

"Got none," he said.

I depressed the button on the Handie-Talkie and spoke into it. "Come in Nancy Drew," I said. "Nancy Drew come in."

"Cute," she said. "You gotta plan?"

"I guess you could call it that."

"Am I in it?" she asked.

"You have the most important part," I said. "Walk over to Lauren, tell her she's in danger and that I asked you to take her home, then do. Clip and I are gonna try to jump the guy who's following her."

"Are you sure I'm ready for such a *big* assignment, Jimmy?"

"I believe in you, Nancy. I really do."

"Seriously, Jimmy, why won't you let—"

"Dammit, July—" I began, but stopped when she turned off her radio.

"Go see if you can find her," I said to Clip. "I'll keep an eye on Lauren until you get back."

"Okay," he said, "but I think she can handle herself just fine."

Watching Lauren as she continued to wander around aimlessly, an unseen weight pressing down on her, I was filled with conflicting thoughts and feelings. How could one person make me feel so many different things?

Searching the vicinity around Lauren to see if July might actually be doing what I had asked her to, I saw movement in the tall stalks of bamboo next to the path in the far corner. Lauren was heading directly toward it.

I eased in the direction of the bamboo thicket, moving slowly, staying in the shadows, and was about halfway there before Lauren reached it. If the person in the thicket was July or even the guy following her just trying to get a better look, I didn't want him to know I was here, but I wanted to be close enough to respond quickly if something went down.

And it did.

As Lauren reached the thicket, a man sprang out of the bamboo, pounced on her, and drug her back in with him.

Chapter 30

It all happened so fast I wasn't sure it had happened at all. It was quiet, too. Neither Lauren nor her attacker had made a sound.

I raced toward them, jumping over the benches and tables in my way.

The dim ground was mostly grayish sandy dirt with only the occasional patch of dampening yellowish grass, and in several places crooked oak roots broke the surface of the soil, slowing me down and making me stumble.

When I reached the place where they had disappeared, I didn't slow down, just plowed into the thicket as fast as I could. As I came through, I tripped over something on the ground and fell face first into the dirt, bamboo branches slapping me as I fell.

As soon as I hit the ground, I rolled over and raised my arm to ward off an attack, but none came. As I sat up and looked around I heard small moans. I had tripped over Lauren. She was lying on the ground a few feet away from me, but whoever had pulled her in had vanished.

She wasn't moving that I could tell, but it was so dark that she could have been bleeding to death from a slit in her throat and I wouldn't have known it.

I scrambled over to her, feeling her face and neck.

She was breathing, her pulse pounding in her throat, and I couldn't feel or see any injuries.

"Lauren," I said. "Are you okay?"

"Jimmy?" she asked. "Is that you?"

"Yeah."

"Did you grab me?"

"No," I said, getting to my feet and helping her up. "I tripped over you."

"I was okay until then," she said. "I think you broke a rib."

"Really?" I asked, reaching down and running my fingertips along her side.

"Not literally," she said. "I was kidding."

"Oh," I said. "Sorry."

We stood there awkwardly for a moment, breathing our labored breaths into each other.

"What're you doing here?" she asked.

"A lousy job of protecting you."

"Where's Harry?" she asked. "Is he—"

"He's fine," I said. "Walt and Ray took him home."

"Didn't I tell you not to follow me?" she said.

"Yeah, but you didn't mean it. Besides, aren't you glad I did?"

She smiled. "At the moment," she said. "But I'll be good and mad later."

"Did he say anything to you?" I asked.

She shook her head.

"Did he try to do anything to you?"

She shook her head again.

"Why didn't you scream?"

"Why all the questions?" she asked. "I don't know why. I was scared. He had my mouth covered. I can't remember. It happened so fast."

"So he just dragged you into the woods, dropped you, and ran off?"

"I guess, Jimmy. I'm not sure. I'm in shock at the moment—ask me later."

I heard a rustling in the leaves and bamboo branches behind me and turned around, reaching for my gun.

"Don't shoot me, motherfucker," Clip said, holding up his hands, which were nearly invisible in the dark night.

"I can't even see you," I said.

He laughed, then stopped abruptly and said, "Don't make a colored man feel bad for being dark."

"Where's July?"

"She's coming," he said. "She's right behind me."

"Stay here with Lauren, I'm gonna see if I can find the guy."

As I was leaving, July appeared behind him, her white face only slightly more visible than his. She was breathing heavily, and had a confused, slightly quizzical look on her face.

"You okay?"

She nodded, but quickly averted her eyes from mine.

"What is it?"

She shook her head. "Nothing," she said. "Guess I'm not cut out for fieldwork after all. Just go."

"Watch them," I said to Clip.

I ran out of the bamboo and back into the park, my eyes scanning the darkness and the lights that dotted it. I was searching for movement.

I saw none.

Giving up on seeing him, I closed my eyes and stood there in the stillness and quiet, only the sounds of crickets in my ears, and listened for him.

My attention was first drawn to the small splash of a fish jumping in the lake, then to the deep guttural groan of a bullfrog or a gator—I wasn't sure which—and to the rustling of bamboo stalks further down the woods from where he had snatched Lauren.

I took off toward the sound, the dried acorns and brittle oak leaves crunching under my feet sounding like car tires on an oyster shell parking lot.

The noise must have warned him of my approach. When I stopped at the edge of the woods, the yellow and green bamboo stalks in front of me were still and quiet.

After waiting for another moment and not hearing or seeing him, I decided to get ahead of him and circle back. I ran along the path about twenty feet further, then turned into the woods, heading back in the direction I had heard him.

This time it was he who heard me. He shot out of the bamboo like a jackrabbit, running across the park toward its exit, darting around the objects in his way.

Rather than chase him, I ran straight up the side of the park, sprinting toward the gate. It worked. I got there before he did. When he saw me, he stopped abruptly and ran the other way. I followed.

Running down the slope toward the water, I was unable to gain on him.

As he neared the water, Clip appeared to his left, which caused him to pause for a moment. I caught up with him then, and when he started to run again I was right behind him.

We were beneath cypress trees now, the lake just a few feet away. When he got near a small group of cypress knees sticking up about two feet out of the ground, I shoved him and he tripped over them and went head first into the lake.

He immediately tried to swim away, but I dove on top of him, wrestling him to the shallow bottom and holding him there until he submitted.

When he surrendered, I pulled him up and pushed him toward Clip, who was standing at the water's edge. Not wanting to get wet, he sidestepped the man and pushed him to the ground.

I waded out of the water, panting and gasping.

"Stick him in your trunk," I said between gasps, "and we'll have a little sit down with him after we get the ladies home safely."

Lauren and July called to us from a short distance away.

"Where are you guys?" July asked.

"Smile for them," I said to Clip, then yelled to July, "Just follow Clip's smile."

For the first time since we had been in the park, a small breeze blew in, rippling the surface of the lake and waving the Spanish moss in the oaks above us as a few loose leaves drifted to the ground. The edges of the breeze held the slightest hint of the approaching winter and I shivered slightly in my wet clothes.

When the two women walked up, Lauren stepped around July and kicked the man on the ground in the ribs. He yelped but still didn't look up.

An acorn falling from one of the tall oaks banged into the roof of the pavilion and it made a loud popping sound like a small caliber revolver. We all jumped. Clip drew his gun and spun around toward it.

"It's an unarmed acorn," I said. "Don't shoot."

Lauren laughed, and for a moment, just a moment, everything seemed okay.

"Let's go have a talk with this guy," I said. "July, would you make sure Mrs. Lewis gets home safely?"

"Sure," she said, her voice distant, distracted.

"Are you sure you're okay?" I asked. "You seem a little shaken up. Did something happen out there?"

"No," she said, shaking her head. "I just wish I had been able to help more. Wish you'd let me do more and not be so damned overprotective. I'm going. I'll talk to you in the morning."

She walked away, Lauren remained with us, and we all stood there in silence for a moment.

"What the hell is going on?" I said.

"With her?" Clip asked.

"With everything," I said.

He smiled. "Maybe you should hire a detective to find out."

Chapter 31

"**If** I want someone watching me," Lauren said, "I'll hire someone I *haven't* slept with."

"Would you be able to find anyone?" I said.

We were walking toward my car, which was back at the school.

She didn't say anything, just looked down and reached into her pocket. When she looked up again there were tears in her eyes.

"Sorry," I said. "I didn't mean—"

"The point is, if I need help you're the last person I need it from."

"Why?"

"It doesn't matter," she said. "If I need help, I'll hire someone. My husband is very wealthy."

I smiled. "He certainly is," I said. "Have him use some of it to hire someone soon."

"Didn't you catch him tonight?" she asked.

"We caught someone," I said. "But I doubt it'll end your troubles, will it?"

"Will you just . . . "

"What?" I asked.

"Call me a cab."

"No," I said. "It won't kill you to slum a little. Now quit being so silly and get in."

We rode to her house in silence, my mood dropping with my adrenaline levels, anger and awkwardness joining my jitters and the thick tension in the car.

I wanted to pull the car off on one of the side roads, park, and force her to tell me what was going on. Thinking of that made me want to do other things in the dark, parked car, too. I wanted to overpower her, take off her clothes, smell her, feel her, taste her again.

When we reached downtown and neared Beach Drive and the waterfront mansion that had been in her husband's family as long as their bank, I said, "Why'd Harry drop out of the race?"

"He didn't," she said. "And he's not going to. And anyway, I told you to stay out of—"

"Actually, you asked me to *help* Harry," I said, "which is what I was doing tonight when he made the announcement."

"You're right," she said. "I'm sorry."

"Please drop me off here," she said when we were still a few houses down from hers. "Please. I don't want to have to explain anything to Harry or . . . anyone else."

"Who?"

"His campaign manager and head of security."

"Harry knew we were looking for you," I said. "Besides, sounds like there's not going to be a campaign."

"Please," she said.

I pulled over and parked in front of a red brick home with a huge plate glass Florida room overlooking the bay. The enormous old oaks in the yard were dark and wouldn't be lit from beneath again until after the war.

"All I want to do is help you," I said.

"That's all?" she asked.

"Well," I said, "maybe not *all*, but I *do* want to protect you."

The neighborhood was quiet the way wealthy neighborhoods are, the bay calm, the faint slice of moonlight streaking across its still surface, the green channel markers stretching across its length, flashing like a small airport runway in the middle of the night.

"I shouldn't have asked you to help Harry," she said. "I don't know what I was thinking. I think it's best if he gets someone else."

"It's not Harry I'm concerned about," I said. "Why am I the last person to help you?"

She reached for the door handle. "I've got to go."

"Why?" I asked. "Why won't you let me help you?"

She opened the door, the light coming on to reveal our dirty and disheveled conditions, and got out. "I just can't," she said, eased the door shut, ran down the sidewalk, up her driveway, and back into her prison.

Chapter 32

When I arrived at the empty warehouse in St. Andrews, Ray and Clip were already working on the guy who had grabbed Lauren.

The dusty old building was dark except for the single floodlight illuminating their work area and empty except for a few wooden crates and some trash scattered throughout. Standing there in the darkness, only the occasional burst of sound echoing through the vast space felt more like being on a Hollywood sound stage than a vacant warehouse in the Florida Panhandle.

Not wanting to break their flow, I hung back and studied the little man from the cover of darkness the way he had Lauren earlier in the evening. He was a small man with pale skin and the beginnings of a potbelly.

He sat in a straight-back wooden chair, his hands tied behind him, his body slumping forward against the rope around his chest.

His face was red and puffy, his right eye swollen shut, and a steady trickle of blood dripped from his left nostril. It was obvious they had already put him through his paces, and I wondered how much more he could take.

When Ray spotted me he walked over to where I stood, as Clip continued to punch the man with his glove-covered fists, all the while whispering in his ear.

"How'd Clip find you?" I asked.

I had called Ray from the school when I went back to get my car, but hadn't gotten an answer.

"He didn't," he said. "I found him. After we got Lewis home, I drove around downtown looking for you or Mrs. Lewis and found Clipper."

Clip started slapping the man hard across the face with his open hand and he let out a little yelp the way puppies do when an older dog finally gets tired of their playfulness and nips at them.

"This guy's just about ready to go," Ray said.

Overhead the exposed rusty beams supporting the roof were caked with dust and wrapped with cobwebs.

The man began to cry, sobbing between his pleas.

Clip turned to us and said, "Carl here has something he wish to say."

We walked over to them.

"That didn't take long," Ray said.

I stood directly in front of Carl and looked down at him intently. "Let's hear it."

"Tonight was the first night I followed that lady," he said. "I swear to God."

"We already know that," Clip said. "You been there before we'd've caught your ass sooner."

Carl looked at me, his eyes searching mine. "So you believe me?"

"Why were you following her tonight?"

"I was hired to," he said. "I swear it."

"By whom?"

"Her husband."

"What exactly did her husband hire you to do?" I said.

"Watch her," he said. "Follow her around. Said somebody was harassing her. If anybody messed with her, stop them."

"That's it?"

"Yeah."

"So why'd you pull her into the bushes?"

"I was trying to protect her," he said. "I saw you guys and I thought she was in real danger. I pulled her in and tried to explain what I was doing, but she fought me. When she pulled a little pistol out of her purse, I ran."

Ray pulled the small leather sap out of his pocket, and the little man's eyes grew wide.

"Come on, fellas," he said. "I'm talkin'."

"Yeah, but you're not telling us the truth," I said.

He started to say something, but before he could, Ray began to work on him with the sap. He was good with it, and it wasn't long before Carl was crying again—and swearing to tell the truth this time.

"I was hired to scare her and give her a message," he said. "I swear. I can't take no more. I swear I'm telling the truth this time."

"Who hired you?" I asked.

"A guy named James Riley," he said.

Ray and Clip looked at me.

"I look dumb enough to hire him?"

They both nodded.

I looked back at Carl. "Jimmy Riley, huh? Did I hire you?"

He looked confused. "What?"

"My name's Jimmy Riley," I said.

His eyes widened. "I'm not lying," he said. "I swear. The guy said his name was James Riley. I swear that's the truth."

I was inclined to believe him.

"What'd he look like?"

"He was a big guy," he said. "Not fat, but big with muscles. I only saw him once, and that's all I remember. I swear it."

"What was the message?" I asked.

He looked confused for a moment.

"For the girl," I said. "What was the message?"

"Make sure her husband drops out of the campaign or everyone will know."

"Know what?"

"I don't know," he said. "That's all he told me. Stay out of the election or everyone will know."

Chapter 33

By the time I reached Beach Drive the next morning, a taxi, with Lauren in it, was backing out of her driveway. I was thankful I was in Clip's car, which I had rented for this occasion, because when I passed the cab Lauren was looking out the back window right at me.

She was gazing out seemingly lost in thought, and if she recognized me she didn't give any indication, so I pulled in the next side road, turned around, and pulled back into traffic behind them.

A low fog hovering just above the surface of the bay spilled onto the road in small patches that looked like clouds seen from a plane and seemed to soak up the beams of the headlights shining into them. Though there was plenty of light, the sun had yet to rise above the trees on the horizon and burn off the chill in the early morning air.

Ray was camped out at Rainer's sanatorium, waiting for his return. We had stopped by last night after leaving the warehouse and searched the place, but he hadn't been there. We both felt like he had the information we needed, the secrets Harry and Lauren were hiding from us, and we looked forward to the opportunity of making him sing—in fact, there was only one place I wanted to be more than in a small room with Rainer, and that was close to Lauren.

The first place the taxi took Lauren surprised me. I had never known her to be a religious person. We had left God out of our relationship entirely. The guilt she felt over our affair aside, she didn't strike me as a very moral person either. It wasn't that I thought she was immoral. I didn't. Just a typically amoral member of the ruling class. But here she was—attending early Mass at St. Dominic's, the small Catholic church on Harrison Avenue.

She looked out of place in her black sheath dress and silk stockings among the simply attired elderly women she joined—and they noticed, many of them making no attempt to conceal their scrutiny.

When I walked into the back of the sanctuary after the service had started, I received enlightenment. It didn't take a trained investigator to see that the most likely explanation of her newfound religiosity was the priest standing behind the alter.

I had seen him before, though he wasn't wearing his Roman collar at the time. He had been wearing the casual clothes appropriate for a clandestine meeting at the Wakulla Springs Lodge.

I eased out of the church quietly and waited inside Clip's car. I had never liked churches. They always felt more like prisons than anything else to me—even at weddings, but particularly at funerals. It wasn't that I didn't believe in God or find some aspects of religion interesting and amusing, but whatever notion I had of whoever is beyond all this had nothing to do with what went on inside the small wooden churches that littered the landscape of Panama City.

I picked up the paper off the seat beside me and flipped through it. Italy had declared war on Germany. Canadian forces had taken Campobasso. US, British, and Soviet foreign ministers were meeting in Moscow. And after winning the mayoral debate against incumbent Frank Howell, candidate Harry Lewis shocked everyone by announcing that he was seriously considering dropping out of the race.

The Big Goodbye

In the fog-diffused morning light, St. Dominic's seemed to glow as if what I were looking at was an old faded photograph instead of an actual building.

After the service, Lauren and the priest lingered near the door as the old ladies crept to their cars and eased out of the lot. Eventually, he walked her out to her waiting cab. Even from this distance, their body language conveyed intimacy and an easiness with each other that only comes from a lot of time together. Once he had her in the cab, he bent down and kissed her on the cheek, his lips lingering a little too long on her flushed face.

Pulling out of St. Dominic's, the cab edged back into traffic on Harrison, driving slowly, seemingly in no hurry.

Unbidden, thoughts of my relationship with Lauren came and stayed. Before the jealousy, before the breakup, before the obsession, before it all, there had been bliss.

I was overcome with a deep sadness. All at once, I realized just how much I had lost—Lauren, our future, my arm, my career, my future. Everything. All of it. All at once. And I couldn't breathe.

Before I met Lauren, I was only vaguely aware of my discontent and disconnectedness. I had longed for more than my banal existence, but wasn't sure what that would be. Now, having had so much, I was finding it difficult to go quietly back into the night of meaninglessness and mediocrity—I had been awakened and did not want to go back to sleep.

Even in the midst of my bitterness and regret, I couldn't deny what we had experienced. Not even my cynicism could protect me from reality, and no matter how suspicious I was of Lauren now, I still knew she had felt it too, knew she had genuinely loved me. Regardless of how many men came before or how many followed, I knew she had never had with them what we had.

When the cab pulled onto Grace Avenue, I realized I hadn't been back to see Ann Everett like I promised her I would. I needed to schedule an appointment—and actually keep it. But my hollow heart sank when Lauren's cab parked in front of her office and she went inside.

Is she seeing us both? How could she? That would be . . . The things she must know about us, I thought. Seeing us both—she's the only person in the whole world who knows the whole story.

I grew angry as I realized that she knew more than I did. She knew why Lauren had left me. She knew Lauren's hidden self, the secret depths I had yet to dive.

She also knew many of my secrets. She knew how seeing Lauren again had affected me. She knew I was following her. She knew—what if she were telling Lauren?

How could she not think we'd eventually bump into each other as we came and went from her office or find ourselves seated across from each other in the singular silence of a shrink's waiting room?

I thought about what to do.

I got out of my car and walked to the service station on the corner and used the payphone to call Everett.

"I've got to speak to Ann," I said in a panicked, breathless voice when the receptionist answered the phone. "Right now."

"She's in a session right now," she said. "Can I take a—"

"It's an emergency," I said. "I've got to talk to her right now."

"Sir, I'm sorry, but—"

"It's a matter of life and death," I said, and gave her my name. That did it.

"Hold on just a moment."

In less than fifteen seconds, Ann Everett was on the line. Lauren must have been in the room with her because she didn't say my name and she had a dry, pinched quality to her voice I had never heard before.

"I need to see you," I said.

"Sure," she said. "I'll have Midge set up something soon."

"Right now," I said. "I've got to see you. Can't wait."

"I can't right now," she said. "I'm with a client and I've got—"

"I'm coming. I'll be there in a few minutes."

172

"What?" she asked in shock. "No, now's not good. Really, you shouldn't. Wait. Let's schedule you for—"

"I have to," I said and hung up.

Lauren came out a few minutes later, got into her cab, and rode away. I smiled to myself as I pulled out onto the road and followed her.

When the cab dropped her at her home, I suddenly had time to see Ann Everett, which I did.

"**W**here have you been?" Ann Everett asked. "You said it was an emergency. I cleared my schedule. What took you so long to get here?"

"I didn't have any intention of coming," I said. "I was following Lauren. When I learned that you were seeing both of us . . ."

"Oh," she said, obviously taken aback.

"I unexpectedly got a moment and decided to see what you had to say for yourself."

She nodded slowly. "I'm sorry."

"All the answers I've been searching for, all the reasons, all the explanations—everything I was stumbling around trying to find— you knew all the time. You knew more than anyone. You were the only person on the planet who had both sides of the story. You knew everything and you didn't even let on that you knew *her*."

"I couldn't," she said. "I'm sorry, but I just couldn't."

Her blonde hair was still flipped out, her black-rimmed glasses in place, and though she still looked like a co-star, her now veiled eyes and guarded face would prevent her from playing the girl next door or the virtuous, worshipful wife.

"You could've said *something*," I said. "Told one of us you couldn't see us or—"

"There was no conflict for me," she said. "I—"

"Enjoyed our little Saturday matinee melodrama," I said. "It gave you a sense of power over us, of control."

"I realize you're upset," she said. "And I understand, but don't let that cloud your thinking. I've provided good counseling to you both. I've not done anything unethical or—"

"We'll see what the ethics review board says about that," I said.

"*What?*"

"I plan to report the situation," I said.

Fear flashed in her eyes and her voice grew tight and pinched like her face. "Jimmy, you're overreacting. I'm sorry you feel betrayed, but the truth is you haven't been. I haven't done anything—"

"What did Lauren tell you?" I asked.

"What? About what?"

"I want to know what she told you—in her sessions."

"I can't reveal that," she said. "You know that."

"Just give me a summary."

She shook her head. "I won't. I would never—"

"Even to save your license?"

"You're threatening me?"

"Actually, it's blackmail," I said.

"I think you need to leave," she said. "I would never do anything that violated the trust of a client."

"You mean beside see their ex-lovers without them knowing it?"

When I left Ann's office, I decided to check in at ours and try to figure out my next move.

My heart started pounding and I grew lightheaded when I rounded the corner at the Tennessee House and saw all the squad cars in front of our building. I parked, jumped out, and ran up to the police line. Ray was just beyond the line talking with Pete.

Pete motioned me in and the patrol cop stepped aside and let me pass.

Ray looked as if he had just stepped off a small boat in a turbulent sea, his pale, expressionless face tinged with green.

"What is it?" I asked.

"They found a body inside," Ray said. "They think it might be July."

Chapter 34

Walking past the uniform stationed at the door, Pete, Ray, and I ducked beneath the crime scene tape and entered our building.

I could tell immediately that the scene was being processed the way it should be. There were enough, but not too many cops around, each doing a specific task. Everything was quiet and orderly—a modicum of respect usually missing. The presence of Henry Folsom, the most senior detective of PCPD, personally ensured that the perp would be apprehended and prosecuted successfully. He wouldn't have it any other way.

"Get your goddamn hands in your pockets," he yelled at a plainclothes detective. "I don't want you touchin' anything."

Henry Folsom was a large man. Everything about him was thick. He was tall and middle-aged, but muscular—only some of which was beginning to turn to fat. As usual, he was wearing his trench coat and fedora inside.

He was standing at the top of the stairs watching as the initial pictures were being taken.

"Jimmy," he said. "How you been?"

He had been my boss at one time. He was a decent man, a tough and honest cop.

"Not bad—unless it's . . . How am I about to be?"

"Not good," he said, shaking his head and frowning, then spoke to Ray.

Ray nodded, but didn't say anything.

Distance. Numbness. Shock. Everything around me receded— further and further until a great distance away—and I could feel nearly nothing. Neither Ray nor I could say much of anything or show any emotion in front of Henry and his men—which wouldn't be a problem for me. I was having a hard enough time just breathing.

We waited in silence for a moment after the pictures were completed for measurements to be taken, drawings to be done—all the while Henry taking down notes on a small pad he pulled out of his jacket pocket.

Though I couldn't see the body from where we stood, most of the activity was taking place in my office.

"Is she in there?" I asked.

Henry nodded very slowly as he continued to scribble onto a pad.

The drawers of July's desk and the filing cabinet behind it were open, manila file folders and papers littering the desktop and floor. I squatted down and peered beneath the desk, praying July's purse wouldn't be in its usual spot. It was.

"Is it there?" Ray asked. "I couldn't bring myself to look."

I nodded, and as I stood, all the blood seemed to drain from my head, and I wobbled slightly until Ray grabbed my arm and steadied me.

"Who found her?" I asked.

Butch had yet to make an appearance, and Pete, though still present, remained silent. There was tension between us, sure, but I suspected he was hoping the way he and Butch had treated me and what

Butch had done to Ray wouldn't come up in front of Folsom—which meant he didn't know anything about it.

"Potential client came in this morning looking for Ray," Henry said.

Ray let out an ironic and bitter burst of laughter, and I knew what he was thinking. Who would hire the services of an agency that couldn't even keep one of its own safe?

"The door was unlocked?" I asked.

"Just as if you were open for business," he said.

Ray was pale, the pain chiseled on his face in deep furrows. He said, "Jimmy and I were out working cases. I tried to call her a couple of times this morning, but never got an answer. We worked pretty late last night. I figured she'd come in later."

"And the last time either of you saw her alive was . . ."

"Late last night," I said. "We were working a case until—"

"I'll need you to tell me that one in detail."

I did—well, most of the details anyway, grateful to have something to concentrate on.

Unlike July's work area, nothing in my office had been disturbed. Everything was just as I had left it—stacks of books scattered throughout the room amidst dusty framed photographs on the floor, a chess set, a phonograph with records—only now July's body was seated in my chair, her pretty face bruised and bloody, her lifeless eyes staring out at nothing.

"Why put her in here?" Henry asked. "Why in Jimmy's chair?"

I didn't say anything.

"It's obviously a message," Ray said.

"To me?"

"Maybe, but probably to both of us. Two offices, one body. Just happened to pick yours."

"Then why not put her in her own chair? Be more shocking to walk in and see her first thing. And he had to think one of us would be the first to see her."

Ray nodded.

"We thinking revenge from a spouse who was on the wrong side of one of your lenses?" Henry asked.

"Or a warning from someone we've yet to expose," I said.

"The first's a pretty long list," Ray said. "The second one's not."

"Speaking of which," Henry said. "Guess which Chester made bail this morning?"

"*Stanley Somerset?*" Ray and I asked simultaneously.

"Uh huh," he said. "What I hear, you guys robbed him of his one chance at true love."

This wasn't the work of Stanley Somerset. It was too close to the MO of the guy who did Freddy, Margie, and Cab, but it wouldn't hurt any to let Henry think it could be. Let him look for Stanley while we found the dead man who did this to July.

"Ah, Detective," the coroner said from somewhere behind us.

We turned toward him.

"The guy you're talking about couldn't have done this," he said.

Henry shot us an amused look. "Oh yeah?" he said. "Why's that?"

"Because," the tech said, "this young lady was killed some time last night."

Chapter 35

"Why the hell did she go back to the office so late?" Ray asked.

I didn't have an answer, so I asked a question of my own. "Do you think she was followed from the park?"

"Almost had to have been," he said. "How would anyone else even know where she was?"

I nodded.

"She was mad at me when she left," I said.

"Got nothing to do with this," he said. "Don't even start down that road."

I had thought once we were away from the other men, we might grieve—at least a little, but as in all things I deferred to Ray, followed his lead.

We had walked down the stairs, past the cops, headed down Harrison, and were now beneath the large vertical THEATER sign of the Ritz.

"You know *we've* got to be the ones to catch him," he said. "Our own secretary in our own building."

"I wanna do more than catch him," I said.

He nodded, then abruptly stopped walking.

"Where are we going?"

"I'm not sure," I said. "I guess I was just getting away from it."

All around us, people were lined up along the sidewalks, straining to see what the police were up to. Standing in small groups, the crowd composed mostly of women, they whispered to each other in hushed, but excited voices.

"I've got to be in court in a few minutes," he said. "When I get a break, I'll track down Rainer."

I nodded.

"What about you?"

"Think I'll pay another visit to the Lewises," I said. "I'll be shocked if this isn't connected to them somehow."

"**W**here's your wife?" I asked.

"I'm not sure," Harry said. "She's not here."

I pushed past him without being invited, stepping into Lauren's other world, the one I had always been excluded from.

"Where is she?"

"I honestly don't know," he said. "I came home for lunch and she was gone."

"What the hell is going on?" I said.

"I'm afraid I'm going to have to ask you to leave," he said.

"No need to be afraid," I said. "Ask all you like, but I'm not going anywhere until I start getting some goddamn answers. People are dying all around us—at least one that I really cared about. So no more lies, no more denials, no more time to be polite."

As I had suspected, Harry had provided a plush prison for his child bride. Their mansion was filled with the finest furniture and the most exquisite accessories a banker's money could buy. It made me simultaneously sick and angry, and I couldn't decide if I wanted to vomit or bust the place up.

"What people?" he asked. "Who's dying?"

"Our secretary for one," I said. "Girl named July."

"And you think that has something to do with me or my wife?"

"Yeah," I said. "Just like the deaths of Freddy Moats, Margie Lehane, and a gunsel named Cab."

"Sir, I assure you I don't know any of those people, except Margie vaguely, of course, and wouldn't have any idea why they were killed."

"Probably has something to do with why you dropped out of the race," I said.

"I haven't dropped out yet," he said. "I may not."

"Why are you even considering it?"

"It's a very personal matter," he said. "Extremely private."

I shook my head. "Not anymore."

"I really don't think you—"

I drove my left fist into his soft, old man's belly. He doubled over, gasping for breath. I had dreamed of doing that and more to him for a long time, but it was no good. There was no pleasure in it.

It took a moment, but he stood upright again.

"You're gonna beat up a helpless old man?"

"That and a lot worse if I have to," I said. "Somebody came into our office and killed our secretary—propped her up in my chair, put her on display—a girl who was doing what she could to protect you and your wife. Now tell me what the fuck's going on?"

"I don't know," he said. "I swear."

I hit him again, another shot to his gut. I didn't want to really hurt him if I didn't have to, didn't want to mark up his face or do any damage anywhere that could be seen—not that I could do much damage with my left anyway.

He doubled over again, but this time he didn't stop. Dropping to his knees, he grabbed his stomach and tried to get some air.

"Why're you dropping out of the race?" I asked.

It took him a moment, but eventually he managed a weak, "For Lauren."

"Why?"

"She wouldn't tell me," he said.

I waited, letting him take in some more air.

"A man calling himself Eisler told me that if I didn't drop out of the race he'd go public with information and evidence about my wife that would not only disgrace and humiliate both of us, but would ensure I'd lose anyway."

"And you just took his word for it?"

"Of course not," he said. "I asked Lauren if there was anything to it, and she said there could be. She told me she might be able to make it all go away, to give her a few days. So I did."

"Which is when all the bodies began dropping."

"Lauren wouldn't—"

"Any idea what this Eisler has on her?"

He shook his head. "Mr. Riley, my wife and I are—well, our relationship is . . . not typical. I can't imagine what he's got, but it must go way beyond simple infidelity."

"When has infidelity ever been simple?" I said.

"That's all I know," he said, "except for one other thing—and I know it for sure. Lauren may be guilty of various indiscretions, but she is not mixed up in murder."

"You don't even know what's going on," I said. "How can you be sure she's not behind the murders?"

"Because I know Lauren," he said, "and if you knew her, you'd be just as certain. Besides, didn't someone tell me that all the recent victims you mentioned had been beaten to death? Surely, you can't think any woman capable of that."

"Of course not," I said. "People like you and your wife never do your own dirty work, but in my book, the one who gives the order is just as guilty as the one who pulls the trigger. Maybe more so."

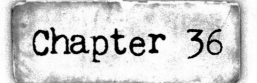

Chapter 36

"You're Jimmy?" Father Keller asked.

"Yeah."

We were standing outside his church on Harrison Avenue. He had been sweeping the front steps when I arrived. The church was empty and silent—inside and out, mine the only car in the lot.

He nodded to himself and examined me closely.

"What?"

"Nothing," he said.

"*Something*," I said.

"I'm sorry. It's just nice to finally meet—you were at Wakulla Springs."

I nodded. "I take it Lauren mentioned me to you."

"*Mentioned?*" he said. "You're all she talks about."

I narrowed my eyes in a look of disbelief.

"I'm serious," he said. "Come inside."

We entered the creaking old church, lit only by candlelight, the flickering shadows from hundreds of votive candles dancing on the walls like the disembodied worshipers of a far more primitive religion.

Walking down the center aisle of the dimly lit sanctuary, I nearly tripped over him when he stopped abruptly to genuflect.

I had believed we were headed to his office, but when he got up, he continued to the front pew and took a seat.

Sitting down next to him, I said, "Tell me about your relationship with Lauren."

"Why don't you ask her?"

"She's missing again," I said.

His eyes widened in what seemed to be genuine surprise. "She is?"

"Looks like it," I said.

Lewis had discovered that Lauren's suitcase and some of her clothes were missing, and he and I had checked everywhere we could think of throughout most of the afternoon, but had not been able to find her.

"You have no idea where she is?" he asked.

I shook my head. "I was hoping you might help me with that."

He frowned. "Wish I could."

"You can start by telling me about your relationship," I said. "You can't be her priest. She's not Catholic. She's not even religious."

"No, she isn't—well, not exactly, but in a weird way I am her priest . . . or at least becoming her priest."

"And you two aren't involved?" I asked.

"Of course we are. We're—"

"I mean intimately."

"*Sexually?*" he asked with a laugh. "No. We're both celibate."

I laughed at that.

"It's true."

"Listen, ah, Father, I'm not here to do you any harm with your church," I said. "I wouldn't know who to report you to and I have no interest in that. So you broke your vows. It's understandable. Lauren's a beautiful, highly desirable woman—"

"I never—"

"I've got to find her," I said. "And the fact that you've got that collar on won't stop me from doing whatever I have to, so don't lie to me. I don't care what you did or why, but you've got to level with me."

"I am," he said. "I was her counselor. I swear before God at this alter. That's all. Her counselor. Nothing more."

"And the hotel room at Wakulla Springs?"

"To ensure privacy," he said. "Which obviously didn't work."

I stared at him, considering whether he was telling the truth.

"If you think I love her," he said, "you're right. If you think I'm attracted to her, you're right, but if you think we've ever done anything inappropriate, you're dead wrong."

I was inclined to believe him. "How long has she been coming to see you?"

"About a year."

"Why'd she start?"

"She had an epiphany," he said.

"A what?"

"An epiphany," he said. "It's a sudden, unexpected special revelation of God."

"And she had one?"

He nodded. "Yeah," he said, a big smile spreading across his face.

"And became religious?"

"Not exactly, no," he said. "She became curious. She was slowly becoming more spiritual, more open to the transcendent aspects of life. She was never interested in anything formal—not doctrine or dogma, she just wanted to understand what happened to her."

"And what was *that?*"

He looked at me with astonishment again. "You don't know?"

"I haven't been a part of her life in quite a while," I said.

He shook his head. "This is so amazing. I just can't get over it. You really don't know."

"There's a lot I don't know," I said. "I'm used to it. It's why I'm here. What I'm not used to is some old priest looking at me like I'm silly."

"I'm sorry," he said. "I really am. I'm just . . ."

"Amazed," I said. "I know."

"Like so many people, she experienced God through another person."

"Another *person*?" I asked, instantly jealous.

"It happens all the time," he said. "A priest, a rabbi, a musician, an artist. For kids it's usually their parents at first, then some sort of hero."

"Who did she—"

"You," he said. "That's why I find it so amazing you don't know."

"*Me?*"

"You," he said. "Well, actually it'd be more accurate to say your love—the love the two of you shared. She was convinced it could have only come from somewhere beyond the two of you."

"What? I don't think . . ."

I shook my head. I just couldn't believe it. It was so incredible. Of course, I had had similar thoughts and feelings about the way we loved each other. I just didn't see them the same way, didn't attribute them to the same thing.

If what he was saying was true, I had been wrong about Lauren, and if I were wrong about this, what else? Were all my perceptions wrong? Just couldn't be. Wasn't possible. I hadn't recovered from the shock of July yet. This was just too, too much.

"You became a metaphor for God for her," he said. "Her epiphany."

I laughed.

"It's true," he said. "Strange, wild, unexpected, unlikely, but profoundly true."

"Not sure what you're selling or why, but I ain't buying."

"You won't even consider what I'm saying is true?"

Could it be? Was it even possible? It seemed more likely Lauren was pulling one over on him.

When I didn't say anything, he added, "It happens more than you think."

"With adulterous lovers?"

"Actually, yes," he said. "Though we'd rather that one not get out. But in a way, that was the problem, wasn't it? Paradoxically, it was you—your love—that made her unable to be with you. It changed her—*God* changed her through you."

"She felt guilty."

He nodded. "And confused. It was a very profound experience and it took her totally by surprise."

"You're saying God took her away from me," I said.

"Well . . ."

I shook my head. "I couldn't believe that if I wanted to—and I don't. I just want to find her."

"And you need to," he said. "As fast as you can. Lately, it wasn't just her epiphany that brought her to me. It was the fact that everything else she tried had failed her."

"Such as?"

"Psychology. Medicine."

"Is she sick?"

"I can't break the seal of the confession," he said, "but—"

"You're doing all right so far," I said.

"So far I haven't told you anything she told me in confession."

"Think about all the times you've spent together," I said, "what she told you about what was going on in her life, in her head. Where did she go? What did she do? Think back to all of that."

"Okay," he said, narrowing his eyes and furrowing his brow in concentration.

"Now," I said. "Where is she?"

Without hesitating, he said, "If anyone else were asking, I'd have said with you."

Chapter 37

The little house on Grace Avenue where Ann Everett had spent so many hours listening to dopes like Lauren and me was easier to break into than I had thought it would be, and I was inside within a minute.

Entering through the back door, I walked down the dark hallway, my flashlight illuminating recently mopped linoleum and reflecting off the glass of the framed diplomas that touted her qualifications.

I was still haunted by the things the priest had said. How could I process it? What could I do with it? There was nothing to do but find her.

Inside Ann Everett's office, I went straight to the filing cabinet I had seen her withdraw and return my file to so many times, picked the lock, which took a lot longer these days, and rifled through the folders until I found one labeled: Lewis, Lauren. I could tell the minute I tugged on it that it was empty, but I pulled it out and looked in it anyway. I was right. Its contents had been removed.

I sat down at Ann's desk and thought about where she might have hidden the accumulated materials from Lauren's sessions. I let my mind drift, keeping it open and unfocused, concentrating on nothing, listening to everything that passed through it. Random thoughts of Lauren, sweet and surprising, counterbalanced images of July's death pose and the enormous hole in me the absence of both women had created.

After searching all the drawers of Ann's desk, I wandered around the small house in the dark, beginning a room by room search.

As I looked around, my mind continued to roam.

What if the person who killed July had Lauren? Did July see, hear, or uncover something about Lauren's real stalker—who had not been Freddy or Carl—that we missed? Was she killed to avoid exposing someone? Would solving the murder reveal the abduction? Or were we dealing with two murders and just hadn't found Lauren's body yet?

I had checked with Ray before coming here. Lauren wasn't at the sanatorium and Rainer had yet to make an appearance either.

As I continued to search, I thought about how helpless Harry had looked sitting there in his estate on the Bay, his millions unable to solve his problems or save his wife. I felt sorry for him, guilty for hitting him.

Thinking of Harry and Lauren forced me to face how utterly inane my perceptions, assumptions, and deductions had been. I had misunderstood, misperceived, and just plain missed everything. A woman who worked for me had been killed and the woman I loved had been kidnapped or killed, and I was stumbling around in the dark as impotent and imperceptive as ever.

I wasn't sure I believed what Father Keller had told me, but I couldn't shake it either. Just the possibility of it haunted me like few things in my life.

Near the back of the house, I found a closet filled with built-in cabinets. As I moved the beam of my flashlight over them I saw they all had hasps and padlocks on them.

A few minutes later, when I had picked the locks, I discovered what was inside. Every cabinet was filled with the recordings of her sessions—not just the early sessions she had asked me if she could record for her project, but every session, all labeled and dated, coded to missing case notes. There weren't enough records for her to have recorded the sessions of all her clients, but she had secretly recorded every session Lauren and I had ever had inside her office.

Taking all the records from our sessions, I walked back into the front room next to the office and placed one of Lauren's on the phonograph.

My eyes stung as Lauren's voice filled the room.

"Have you ever been in love with someone so much that you finally understood what God meant by all of this?" Lauren asked.

"This isn't about me," Ann said. "But all what?"

"Everything," she said. "Life. I know this isn't about you, but how can you help me if you've never experienced what I'm talking about?"

"No, I haven't," Ann said, "but I don't doubt that that kind of love exists."

There was a long pause, and then Lauren said, "That might be enough."

"I think it's more than you'll get from most counselors," she said. "Why don't we give it a try? If it doesn't work, you can try to find someone else who has experienced such love."

"Okay," Lauren said.

As glad as I was to have found the recordings, and as good as it was to hear Lauren's voice, it was also eerie and unnerving to hear it alone in the dark, empty house.

"I am right in assuming you've experienced such a love?" Ann asked.

"Very recently, yes."

"And you've lost it even more recently?"

"What makes you say that?"

"Isn't that why you're here?"

"Not lost as much as gave up."

"Why?"

"I love him," Lauren said, as if that explained everything.

There was a long silence, then a phone ringing, and then nothing. There was nothing else on the record.

Hoping the others contained far more material, I put another recording on the player.

"I don't know," Lauren was saying, "I just seem to get it now. And it's beautiful. Everything works together so well. It's not the same as the eyes of infatuation. I'm aware of the suffering and the horror—but I see the big picture now. Besides, most of the really unspeakable things, we do to each other.

"It makes me want to do something with my life," she continued. "To be a light. I tried to be that for Jimmy, but he wouldn't let me. He doesn't want anything from me—well, actually, I guess he wants everything. I feel so bad. I've started to explain a dozen times, but he's so angry he won't even speak to me. I was doing this as much for him as for me, but it didn't turn out like I had planned."

"Whatta you mean *for* him?"

"He was so possessive, so obsessed. I knew he had experienced what I had, but he thought I was responsible for it. He thought it was me."

Hearing Lauren's voice filled me with a warmth I couldn't describe, but it also heightened my awareness of her absence. It was as if the part of her that had been inside of me had been ripped out, leaving only an empty cavernous ache at my center.

As I gathered together all the recordings, turned off the phonograph, and prepared to leave, I thought, *I've got to find her. I've got to have her back or*—

There was no *or*. I had to find her.

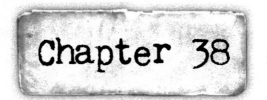

Chapter 38

"It's not just that Harry saved my life," Lauren was saying, "I love him. I was so young when we started dating. He's the only man I've ever been with—except for Jimmy. And he's a good man, he really is—especially for one with so much power and money. And he's getting better all the time. I think my experience is having an effect on him, too."

I shook my head in self-disgust as I recalled all the lovers I had pictured Lauren with.

Still unable to sit at my desk in the chair where July was found, I was on the floor of my office listening to Lauren's sessions on my phonograph.

It was the middle of the night, downtown as dark and abandoned as an amusement park in off season. I sat just outside of a small pool of light created by the desk lamp on the floor next to the speakers, trying to be as close to Lauren's voice as I could. My back was to the wall, eyes on the door, hand near my gun at all times. As much as Lauren's voice warmed and comforted me, I knew July's killer or more men where Cab and Mountain had come from could walk in any moment.

"I just feel so schizophrenic," Lauren was saying now. "Sometimes I'm filled with such guilt and regret, other times with pure gratitude. Sometimes I feel so close to God, others I don't think he even exists, that I've made this whole thing up because I need meaning in my life. Sometimes I want to confess everything to Harry and beg his forgiveness, other times I want to finally leave him forever and be with Jimmy."

What would've happened if she had done that? I would have had no idea of who she really was, of the sacrifice she would have been making, the gift she would have been giving.

My office was intermittently washed in red light as the neon sign for the bar next door cycled on and off against the dark night sky. I stood and walked to the window. When the sign was on, I could see the neon night in light and shadow and nothingness. When it was off, I could see a dim reflection I didn't recognize in the mirror-like glass. The solitary figure looked like the last soldier standing in a world without warmth and light.

The street below was empty except for a few scattered couples, the men in uniform, the women in short, straight skirts. The night was quiet. When there was no sound coming from the recording, the only noise beside my breathing was the low hum and flicker of the neon sign.

"What should I do?" she asked after a long silence.

"What do you think you should do?" Ann asked.

Lauren laughed. "Should I tell Harry?"

"What?"

I walked back over and sat down again.

"That I love Jimmy. That I had an affair. That I'm sorry or I'm leaving or—I don't know. That's why I'm asking. Should I tell him anything at all?"

"Shouldn't you decide first what you're going to do?"

"I guess," Lauren said. "I don't know."

They were both quiet a moment, then Lauren said, "What if I stay with him?"

"Who?"

"Harry," she said. "Should I tell him about Jimmy, about how I felt, how I feel, if I'm going to stay with him?"

"Do you think he'd want to know?"

"I'm not sure."

"What do you think his reaction would be?"

"That of a patient parent," she said. "It's how he treats me most of the time. He's like an indulgent father with me."

"Would he still want to be married to you if he knew how you feel about Jimmy?"

"I can't," Lauren said. "I just can't tell him. He'd still want to be married. We don't have that kind of relationship, but I think it would hurt him. I could no more hurt him than I could Jimmy."

"But you have hurt Jimmy," Ann said.

"Only because I love him."

"Think *he* sees it that way?"

"No, I know he doesn't. Should I tell him? I was so dazed when I left him I don't think I explained anything. The truth was I didn't know what the hell was going on. Still don't most days."

"Would it help him to know?"

"He hates me so much," Lauren said. "I don't think he'd even talk to me. He's so—*maybe* I'm wrong. Maybe he didn't experience what I did."

Ann said something else, but I couldn't make it out, and the recording ended. I snatched it off the turntable and put on another one.

"It's more a feeling than anything else," Lauren was saying, "but I think someone's following me."

"Really?"

"I think it might be Jimmy."

"Wasn't he injured recently?" Ann asked. "Lost an arm or something?"

You know damn well I did. You were treating me at the time.

Lauren must have nodded and begun to cry because there was a pause, then sniffles. "I haven't seen him," she said. "He always told me if he ever followed me I'd never know it."

"But you do?"

"No, I feel it. I sense him."

"If it is Jimmy, why do you think he's doing it?" Ann asked.

"He still hasn't found what he's looking for, I guess," Lauren said. "Must still think it's me."

"Is it?"

"Partly, I guess, but . . ."

"But what?"

I couldn't make out the rest of the recording.

As much as I wanted to hear Lauren's every word, learn what she had been thinking and feeling over the past year when I had been so wrong about what she had been thinking and feeling and doing, I had to find her, so I skipped ahead to a much later recording.

When I put the record on the player, there was nothing but a hiss. Flipping it over, I leaned back, closing my tired eyes, and listened.

"I haven't been feeling good lately," Lauren was saying. "I wonder if I'm depressed?"

"Tell me about it?"

"No energy, no strength, no drive. I don't know, I just don't really feel like doing anything—and I'm not doing as much as I usually do."

Ann didn't say anything and they were both silent for awhile.

"Why don't you see a doctor?" Ann asked.

"With Harry running for mayor I have to be very careful about who I see," she said.

"I have just the person," Ann said.

I sat up.

"His name is Dr. Payton Rainer," she said. "He has a very private facility and he is very discrete."

"I don't know," Lauren said.

"Trust me," Ann said.

Lauren had, and that had been her mistake.

Chapter 39

"I'm not sure I should see you anymore," Lauren said.

"Really?" Ann asked. "Why not?"

"I don't see that it's doing any good," she said. "And it seems so narcissistic to spend so much time talking about myself."

"Narcissistic?"

"Jimmy turned me into a reader when we were together—well, actually I really didn't start until after we were over, but—"

"Well," Ann said, her voice calm, but very cool, "the decision is yours, of course, but I feel like we have made very good progress. You've come a long way in a short time."

"I've been talking to a priest," Lauren said, "and it seems to be helping."

"I see," she said. "Why a priest?"

"No one else can help me now."

"What does that mean?"

"Don't you know?" Lauren asked.

"No, that's why I asked," Ann said.

"I'm sorry," she said. "It doesn't matter."

"Tell you what," Ann said. "Just to make sure this isn't a rash decision, let's schedule two more sessions. Then if you still wish to discontinue therapy I'll support you."

"Okay."

They said a few more things I couldn't make out, then there was a pause.

"So," Ann said. "See you next Thursday."

"Oh, no I can't. Next Thursday I have a doctor's appointment."

"Is it with Dr. Rainer?" she asked. "Did you make it during our time because you intended to discontinue our sessions? How long have you been planning this?"

"It was the only time he could take me," she said. "And it can't wait."

"I hope it's nothing serious," Ann said, fishing.

Lauren didn't respond.

"I guess I thought, given enough time, my desire for Jimmy would wane, my resolve to stay away from him strengthen, but . . ."

"But what?"

"It hasn't turned out that way. In fact, just the opposite. My desire has intensified and my resolve has waned."

"I see."

"Sometimes I want to forget about everything else—God and all the rest—and just be with Jimmy. What does that mean? Am I really supposed to be with him? Have I made a horrible mistake?"

"What do *you* think it means?"

Lauren laughed at that, but it was ironic and humorless. "You've got the easiest job in the world. Just sit and listen, and when asked a question just turn it around on the person and ask them the same thing."

"It's not really me you're angry with, is it?" Ann asked.

"No."

"So," she said again, "what do *you* think it means?"

"I don't know," Lauren said. "I wish I did. I'm just confused and I feel bad. Why does all this have to be so hard?"

I thought about how often I had taken the path of least resistance, never even pausing to consider other roads. Lauren's struggle showed her depth, her growth—just how wrong I had been about her.

"What's really bothering you, Lauren?" Ann asked.

"What a stupid question," she said. "Talk about—"

"What did you find out at the doctor?"

Lauren burst into tears.

I listened for a long time after that, but there was nothing else on the recording.

"You set me up," Lauren said.

"What?"

"You sent me to Rainer," she said. "You're in it with him."

"In what?" Ann asked. "What are you talking about?"

"Don't act like you don't know," Lauren said. "He's blackmailing me."

"*Dr. Rainer?*" Ann asked.

"Yeah."

"For what?"

Lauren didn't say anything.

"What does he have on you, Lauren?"

Lauren still didn't respond.

"Lauren," Ann said. "Tell me what Dr. Rainer has on you."

As Ann continued to press Lauren, I realized she was in on it. She was trying to get Lauren to say what it was so she would have a recording of it.

"Lauren, don't leave," Ann was saying. "Let me help you. You need my help."

The last recording was from this morning. It was the session I had interrupted.

"I've come to beg you," Lauren said. "Not for me, but for Harry. Being mayor is all he's ever wanted, and he'll make a great one. Please, for him, for this town. Please stop what you're doing. I'll pay you anything you like."

"I'm sorry," Ann said. "There's nothing I can do. I wish there was, but there's just not."

"How can you be so . . . cold?" Lauren asked. "People's lives are at stake."

"Don't take it so personal," Ann said. "It's not, you know? Personal, I mean. It's just politics."

"It is personal," Lauren said. "You're killing me, you're robbing Harry of the only thing that matters to him, and you're robbing this great town of a leader worthy of her."

"You seem very calm about all this," Ann said.

"I'm not calm," Lauren said. "I'm very angry. I just don't feel good. I'm having chest pains and I don't have any strength."

"Lauren, listen to me," Ann said. "One way or another Harry's hopes of being mayor are over. Just accept that and go get treatment while there's still time."

Ann's receptionist interrupted then, said it was an emergency. Ann took the call, and Lauren left.

Chapter 40

The next morning, with no sleep, no shave, barely a shower, I was parked across the street from Ann Everett's office on Grace Avenue. I had arrived early, and she was running late. I was hoping that she would walk into her office, see that the recordings were missing, panic, and lead me to Rainer.

Lauren had still not come home. Nor had she shown up at the sanatorium—which Clip was watching while Ray caught a couple hours sleep and a shower.

Everett's first appointment arrived, a short lady with an enormous bottom and some sort of animal on the end of a leash. She parked right in front, whether to show off her importance or to save herself some effort in transporting her backside from the car to the office, I wasn't sure. Probably a combination of both. She got out with whatever was on the leash, shuffled up to the door, and pulled on it. When it didn't give, her hand slipped as she was coming back and she hit the small cement platform with the largest part of her.

After she got up, which took a while, she waited for a few moments then huffed away, dragging the creature on the leash along behind her.

I waited as three other clients arrived, found the door locked, looked around, then left, and was about to give up, when Everett's receptionist pulled up, hopped out of her car, tacked a note to the front door, and took off again.

After reading the note, which said that Dr. Everett was ill and would be out for a few days, I was tailing the receptionist, hoping she would lead me to Everett.

She led me out to Watson Bayou to the new housing complex known as Cove Gardens, which probably meant her husband was an officer stationed at Tyndall Field.

Cove Gardens, a thirty-acre complex located on the old Van Horn homestead, provided one hundred units for non-commissioned officers with the rank of sergeant or above and fifty units for civilian families. Nestled beneath live oaks, surrounded by paved streets and sidewalks, and fronting the waters of Watson Bayou, Cove Gardens offered some of the nicest housing in the area.

Each unit faced the park, so Everett's receptionist parked on the curb and walked into the back of the unit. She didn't knock. In fact, she got in so quickly that I doubted the door had even been locked.

I parked down the street in front of another unit, got out, and walked toward the unit she had gone into, the morning sun dappling the ground beneath my feet, the cool breeze waving the Spanish moss hanging on the oak limbs above.

Standing on the porch next to the 50-gallon fuel tank, I looked around, then tried the door. It was unlocked.

I opened it and went inside.

The units were every bit as nice as I had heard. The kitchen had an electric refrigerator, a bottled-gas range, and a sink and tray combination for washing clothes as well as dishes, which was what I found the receptionist doing.

"Mr. Riley?" she asked. "What are you doing here?"

She twisted toward me, her hands still submerged in the soapy water.

"Don't waste any time, do you?" I asked.

"Huh?"

"Come right in and get to work."

"I was doing the washing when Dr. Everett called and asked me to run an errand for her. What are you doing here?"

"I need to see Dr. Everett," I said.

"She doesn't live here," she said. "This house belongs to me and Richie—my husband. How did you know where I lived? How'd you get in?"

"I followed you from Everett's office," I said. "The door was unlocked, so I came on in."

"Why didn't you knock?"

"I didn't want to interrupt your washing," I said.

"That was—how'd you know I was washing?"

"I've got to see Ann," I said.

She withdrew her hands from the soapy water and began to dry them with a dishtowel that was draped across the back of one of the straight-back wooden chairs around the kitchen table.

"Dr. Everett is taking a few days off for personal reasons," she said.

"I'm sorry," I said, "I've forgotten your name."

"It's Midge."

"Midge, you seem like a nice person, so you're probably not aware of what your boss has been up to—"

"What do you mean?"

"She's mixed up with some very dangerous men in a blackmail scheme."

"Not Dr. Everett," she said. "She couldn't be. She's a healer. She helps—"

"She is," I said. "She's blackmailing one of her clients, Lauren Lewis, to get her husband to drop out of the mayor's race."

Her eyes widened. She knew Lauren was a client, and she had obviously heard about Harry's announcement after the debate.

"Surely there's some mistake," she said. "She would never—"

"She's been recording our sessions without us knowing it," I said.

"I thought you knew," she said. "I thought you had signed a waiver."

"I did," I said. "For just the first few sessions. She told me she was doing research for a project about wounded servicemen. I doubt there's any such project, but even if there were, that was supposed to have ended over six months ago."

She was beginning to entertain the possibility. I could tell.

"It's just all so hard for me to believe," she said.

"That's because you're a good person," I said. "You can't really understand people like Everett and Rainer."

"Dr. Rainer is in on it, too?" she asked.

I nodded. "Midge," I said, "Lauren is very sick and she's missing. I've got to find her and get her some help. Now either Everett and Rainer have her or they know where she is. I've got to find them."

"I believe you. I'd tell you if I knew," she said. "I just don't have any idea. I don't even know where she lives."

"Call her," I said. "Try to get her to let you come by her house or meet you somewhere."

"I couldn't," she said.

"You have to."

"She'd know I was lying," she said. "I'm sorry, but I just can't."

The front door opened and I turned to see an air force uniform full of muscle walk through it.

"What the hell's this?" he asked.

"It's not what you think, honey," Midge said. "I swear it ain't."

"I just need your wife to make a quick phone call for me," I said. "It's extremely important. Then I'll be gone."

"Or you could go now," he said.

"I'll go once your wife makes the call," I said. "I'm not leaving until she does."

"Or maybe you are," he said.

He moved so quickly, there was nothing I could do. In two steps he was right in front of me and in two quick movements, he was smashing a large, heavy ceramic canister into the side of my head.

I was trying to say something, trying to raise my arm to protect myself. I was thinking I could make him understand or catch him off guard, then I was just trying to react, to counter what he was doing, then . . . nothing.

Chapter 41

When I woke up, I was face down on Midge's kitchen floor with a headache and dried blood on my face. Actually, I just thought I had a headache. When I pushed myself up, the real pain began.

"Have a nice nap?"

I looked around to see Butch smiling down at me.

Pete stepped forward, extended his hand, and helped me up. "You okay there buddy?"

I didn't say anything. It was a stupid question. Of course I wasn't okay. I had been whacked on the head with a ceramic canister.

"We got you for breaking and entering," Butch said. "Wanna tell us what the hell you think you're doing?"

I thought about whether I should tell them. It would give them plenty of ammunition to implicate Lauren in all the deaths surrounding the case, but I didn't have a choice. They could help me track down Ann Everett, and that's what I needed to do.

I told them the truth—maybe not the whole truth, but certainly most of it.

Butch turned to Midge, who had been hovering in the background with Richie in the livingroom.

"And you don't know where this Everett woman lives?" Butch asked.

Richie had his arm around the little woman, holding her against his red-blooded, all-American fly-boy body protectively. They looked like an ad for the good life the war effort was protecting.

"No, sir," she said. "I just worked for her. We've never talked about anything personal."

"But you have her number, right?" I asked, adding to Pete, "She's got her number."

"Are you sure about all this, Jimmy?" Pete asked. "You seem like you're—"

"I'm sure," I said. "We've got to find her. And we've got to hurry."

"There's a lot of things I don't like about PIs," Butch said. "A lot. But the thing I don't like the most is how you fellas always make a mess, then we have to clean it up."

"Seems I recall a couple of us cleaning up your mess before you were able to make it recently," I said.

He hesitated, took in a deep breath, and let it out slowly. "Okay," he said, "so I went out of my head for a moment, and you guys helped me. I owe you one. Just don't press it."

I nodded. "I won't," I said. "Just help me find Everett."

Butch looked at Jimmy, who shrugged, then to Midge. "Let's have the number," he said.

She gave it to him. He then borrowed Midge's phone, and called the station while we waited.

"I'm sorry about your head, Mr. Riley," Midge was saying. "I know you didn't mean no harm. My Richie is very protective of me."

"*I'm* sorry I barged in," I said. "I thought you might be involved in this thing with Everett. I wanted to surprise you."

"I understand," she said. "It's okay."

Butch replaced the receiver on the cradle and said, "I've got an address. Let's go see if we can't clean up this mess so you and me can be even."

It wasn't me, but Ray he needed to worry about being even with, but I didn't mention it.

The small block home on Cherry Street in Callaway had obviously been neglected. The yard was mostly dirt with a few tall weeds. Peeling paint flaked off the block and collected in the dirt and weeds on the ground below. Newspaper had been taped over missing window panes and trash spilled out of a tin can in the front corner of the yard.

I had followed Pete and Butch here in my car. I parked behind them on the shoulder of the street and got out.

"You sure this is the right place?" I asked.

"Will you listen to this?" Butch said. "I've got a peeper second guessing me. And not just any peeper, but the one who got us into all this."

"Doesn't look like the lady's home," Pete said, nodding toward the collection of *Herald Tribunes* on the front porch.

"Only one way to find out for sure," I said.

I started to walk toward the house.

"You wait here," Butch said.

"But—"

"I can still arrest you for B and E," he said. "I's you I wouldn't push me."

I knew Midge wouldn't press charges, she wasn't the type, but I held up my hand in a placating manner. "Just hurry."

Moving around Butch, Pete walked much faster to the porch and knocked on the front door. When, after a few moments, there was no response, he knocked again—louder and longer this time. Still nothing. His final knock was not a knock at all but an incessant banging.

"Police. Open up," he yelled.

When there was still no answer, Pete walked around to the back of the house. Butch walked back toward me.

"She ain't here," he said. "We'll come back later."

"But what if—"

"We'll come back later," he said. "Let us run down the rest of your story. Who knows? If we get enough evidence maybe we get a warrant and when we come back it don't matter if nobody's home."

I couldn't figure Butch. He seemed genuine in his attempt to be helpful. Maybe it was his way of repaying me or perhaps he was trying to lull me to sleep in order to set me up somehow, but it seemed like good police work.

"Thanks, Butch," I said.

He grunted.

Pete walked back around and joined us.

"No car," he said. "No sign of life."

"Couldn't we just—"

"You got two choices," Butch said. "Either way we're all leaving this empty house. You can go get your head seen about, get some sleep, clean up—who knows?—maybe even shave, or you can go with us to a nice cozy jail cell. It's up to you."

"Jimmy, we're gonna keep looking for this Everett dame and Rainer, okay?" Pete said. "I'll put out an APB. We'll find them. I promise. Just go get yourself together and let us do our jobs. It's exactly what you would've said back when you was a cop."

I nodded. He was right. "Okay," I said. "I'll go get my head examined."

"Long overdue," Butch said with a mean smile.

"Call me the moment you have anything," I said to Pete.

"Partner," he said, his big blue eyes so innocent and boyish they were almost believable, "you know I will."

I didn't know any such thing, but I needed them to leave so I could break into Everett's house.

"Thanks," I said, nodding, and turned to walk away.

"Peeper," Butch called after me.

I kept walking.

"Don't get any bright ideas," he said. "I'm gonna have this house watched. Midge's place too."

Rubbing the side of my head, attempting to conceal my disappointment, I said, "I think Midge's husband has that covered."

Chapter 42

Butch probably really would have someone watch Everett's place—at least at first. Deciding to wait a while before I broke in, I drove back to the office to test a theory I had about what July might have been doing at the office so late the night she was murdered.

When I pulled up in front of our building, I saw that someone, undoubtably Ray, had placed a wreath on the door. He was the grown-up of this outfit. It hadn't even crossed my mind.

I could tell from the moment I opened the door that the office was empty, and I wondered if it would always be this way. Ray and I were both avoiding it, and I couldn't imagine that we would ever feel comfortable in it again. My guess was when this was all over we'd be looking for a new place.

Walking up the stairs to her work area, a wave of sadness washed over me. She had made this job fun. Unlike Ray, she was easy to talk to and got most of my jokes and references. She was tough and smart—and probably on her way to making a good detective.

As I reached her desk, I wondered again what she was doing here that night. Why come back so late? What couldn't wait until the next morning?

I thought I might just know a way to figure out the answers. Even if I did, it probably wouldn't tell me who killed her, but it'd be a place to start.

Earlier the cops had Ray and me look to see if anything was missing. We had not—at least I had not—looked for what she had been working on. I thought it was possible that whatever was under the files and papers the killer had strewn would tell me.

I began with what was on her desk beneath the files.

Before, we had merely done a cursory check to see if anything was missing, now, I returned everything to its file and stacked them to the side. It took a while, but when I reached the bottom I found what I was looking for—except I didn't like what I had found because it pointed to me. July had come back here from the park to look at our agency's logs, the paperwork we all used to account for our time and to bill clients.

Ray, the former Pinkerton, operated our agency as if we could be audited any minute. July's primary job was to keep careful records of all our activities—including accounting for all the gas and food ration coupons we used on each case.

The logs she had out started a little less than a year ago and went through the present. They showed, among other things, that following our breakup, I had followed Lauren—often on company time—and had falsified records to cover it. It showed Ray's legitimate work for Harry Lewis in following his wife and the other small jobs we were handling at the time, and every hour we had logged on every job since that time.

She also had the invoices out, and together they showed that I had done extensive surveillance work for an Erich Stevens, a client I had made up to cover the fact that I was following Lauren and had never billed. Detective that she was, July, watching Lauren run around the track in the dark, had deduced that I had followed her before. But why come here? Why did she think it was so urgent? Did she think I was following her again? Of course I was, but did she think that I was the one they couldn't get close to or that I had hired Carl—was she that far ahead of us? Did she think Lauren was in danger? That I was going to eventually hurt her? I hope she hadn't died thinking such things about me.

More recently, her logs were incomplete. There were hours logged with no client, clients with no hours, and several hours unaccounted for. Maybe she had come in to catch up on her bookkeeping. She had to know that Ray would be unhappy if he saw the condition everything was in. He had never once been late turning in a report to her, and she was usually good about accounting for everything once she had it. Was she going through something we didn't know about? Was she killed for something that had nothing to do with the Lewis case or anything to do with our agency? If so, why was she killed the same way the other victims were?

On my way back to Ann Everett's place, I stopped by Rainer's sanatorium to check on Ray, but he wasn't there. It was early evening, the end of day, and Clip was still sitting on the building.

I parked next to him near the service station down from Rainer's and got into the passenger side of his car.

"What the hell happened to you?" he asked.

"I didn't duck fast enough," I said.

"From what?"

"An incoming ceramic canister."

"Shit, man," he said, "side of your face is all . . ."

"You should see the canister," I said. "Where's Ray?"

"Haven't seen him."

"What time was he supposed to be back?"

"'Round noon," he said.

"Six hours ago?"

He nodded.

"And you haven't heard from him?"

"Nah," he said.

Something was wrong. Ray was never late, and had he been able, he would have gotten word to us. Had he met up with July's killer? Had he been detained by Rainer? Was Butch behind his absence? Is that why he had been semi-helpful this afternoon?

"Any sign of Lauren?" I said, nodding toward the sanatorium. "Or Rainer?"

He shook his head. "Place dead."

"Up for a few more hours?"

"Your dime," he said. "Been overtime for four hours now."

"You're worth it, aren't you?"

"Worth a hell of a lot more than that," he said. "More'n your one-arm, broke ass can afford."

"Good thing I'm not too proud for charity."

Chapter 43

If the cops were watching Everett's house, they were doing a damn good job of it. I drove around a few times before I parked a couple of blocks down and walked into her backyard. If I had more time, I'd have been more careful, but I didn't.

The back door was unlocked. When I opened it and went in, no one with a badge and a gun jumped out.

It was dark outside now, and there were no lights on inside. I pulled a small flashlight out of my left coat pocket, clicked it on, and had a look around—a little bit at a time.

In contrast to the exterior, the inside of the house was neat and clean, everything in its place.

The house was small, and it didn't take me long to determine no one was home.

It was furnished modestly, devoid of any of the modern con-veniences Midge enjoyed, and I found it difficult to believe that Ann Everett had ever actually lived here. It was much more likely a hideout or the home of one of her cohorts. The fact that its address matched the phone number Midge had for her didn't mean it was connected to her at all.

There were men and women's clothes hanging in the closet of the only bedroom. I tried to recall if I had seen Everett ever wear any of them, but couldn't remember. The drawers were mostly empty. There was nothing between the box springs and mattress. The medicine cabinet had the barest of essentials. Nothing was hidden in the linen cabinet.

The kitchen cabinets were nearly empty—just a bottle of Snider Catsup, a couple of cans of Heinz Home Style Soup, and a few boxes of GE lamps. It had been a long time since anyone had prepared a meal here. There was nothing in any of the appliances.

There didn't seem to be anything helpful anywhere, so I decided to go.

As I was about to leave, I heard the chimes of the large clock in the living room. I turned to take a closer look at it, moving the beam of my flashlight up and down. Ornate and over six feet tall, the squarish frame had a swinging pendulum on a long chain between two columns in the center, and a round clock face at eye level of a tall person.

The base of the clock had a door with a handle. I opened it. There was nothing in it, but as I studied it, I could tell that the back wall was much more shallow than the depth of the clock. Thinking it might be a false wall with a hidden compartment, I tapped on it. It sounded hollow, but I couldn't get it open, and I didn't have time to figure it out. I stood and kicked it in. It shattered, some of the pieces falling into the cuffs of my trousers, and inside was the large envelope Freddy had given to Lauren on the beach behind the Barn Dance.

My heart started racing as I opened it.

Lauren's medical records and detailed notes were inside.

The first word the beam of my flashlight fell on was a dirty word, the kind that led to blackmail, ended political aspirations, and took lives. Few words were as powerful or as deadly.

It explained Lauren's behavior, even her episode at Wakulla Springs. It explained everything.

Lauren had a disease with virtually no early sign of infection. She had a small, non-painful nodule or lesion, which she had ignored. It has gone away in just a few weeks. But untreated, her disease had progressed to the next stage.

As her lesion was going away, she got a reddish-brown rash on the palms of her hands and the soles of her feet. For a while, she had a fever, swollen glands, a sore throat, weight loss, headaches, and fatigue. Again, it was left untreated, and again, it progressed.

As her rash began to disappear, the infection was still in her body, but there were very few symptoms and no outward signs of the disease, and all the while it was damaging her brain, heart, liver, eyes, bones, and joints.

Lauren had put off going to the doctor for as long as she could—perhaps because of how busy she was with the campaign or maybe because she suspected what it was. When she couldn't delay any longer, she trusted Ann Everett's recommendation of Payton Rainer, who administered a blood test called the Wasserman. But instead of treating her with the arsenic preparation and sulfa-like drug known as Salvarsan 606, he began to blackmail her—not for money, but to remove her husband from the mayoral race.

And Lauren couldn't go anywhere else for treatment.

She had syphilis. Margie had given it to me, and I had given it to her. According to the file, there was no other possible explanation. It had gone untreated, and soon her swollen aorta would rupture and she would collapse and die, which would mean I had killed her.

Chapter 44

I drove to the Lewis home in a heavy fog, sick inside, but trying not to think about what I had done. But it was no good. I had to think about it, take it in. I just couldn't stop. If I stopped, I'd implode— from lack of sleep and fatigue, but most of all from guilt.

Everything Lauren had done, she had done out of love. I thought of all the time I had wasted on petty jealousy, wounded pride, and erroneous assumptions about an innocent woman.

Difficult as it was, I forced myself to think about all the hurtful and hateful things I had thought or said about Lauren. How could I have been so cruel? So stupid? So deceived?

She had risked her own life so that Harry could have his dream, so that she could pay him back some small part of what she felt she owed him.

Father Keller thought she was a saint, and maybe she was. I didn't know about that stuff. What I did know about was human nature, what people were capable of. I had often seen the worst, but in Lauren I had been seeing the best—but, because my experience with it had been so limited, I didn't recognize it when I saw it, when I held it, when it was offering the best of itself to me.

As I knocked on the door of the Lewis house, heat lightening flashed out over the bay, flickering like the filament of an old electric bulb coming to life.

Lewis was surprised to see me. "Mr. Riley. Do you have news of Lauren?"

I shook my head.

His face fell, then he turned and walked back into the house. I followed him.

I felt such guilt at what I had done to Lauren, to them both, that I found it difficult to look at him directly.

"I'm so sorry," I said.

He nodded, and I was pretty sure he thought I was offering my condolences for her being missing or apologizing because I hadn't found her yet.

"Would you like a drink?" he asked.

"Sure," I said. I needed one.

He stepped behind a fully stocked bar and mixed up a couple of drinks without asking what I wanted. His bloodshot eyes and swollen red nose let me know he was way ahead of me. As he prepared the drinks, his hands shook, and I couldn't be sure if it were from age, alcohol, or anxiety.

Above the fireplace, a painting of Lauren in a formal gown hung in an ornate gold frame. The artist had painted her without her scars, and she looked like a model or a movie star, a woman so beautiful that the world must take notice.

We sat on expensive and uncomfortable furniture surrounded by tables and mirrors and vases and lamps and paintings.

Harry looked even older than the last time I had seen him, his blue eyes tired, rimmed with smudges of purplish bruises, and there seemed to be even more broken veins in his pale, puffy face.

"How you holdin' up?" I asked.

He shook his head. "Not well, I'm afraid."

"I'm sorry. I won't keep you long. I just wanted to see if you had thought about anywhere Lauren might've gone."

He shook his head again. "I've thought and thought and just can't come up with anything. I'm afraid we aren't very close in that sense. We've lived separate lives. I'm sorry, but I just don't . . ."

"No obscure friend or relative?" I asked. "No vacation spot she's fond of?"

"None. No one."

He then withdrew a pack of cigarettes from an end table and offered me one.

I declined.

"What have you decided about the election?"

With trembling hands, he placed a cigarette in his mouth and lit it. He then took a long pull on it like someone unraveling, hoping to inhale some steadiness.

"I'm holding a press conference tomorrow," he said. "I'm dropping out of the race."

Without knocking, Walt walked through the front door and into the livingroom. He was still wearing his coat and hat.

"Everything okay, Mr. Lewis?" he asked.

Lewis nodded. "Fine, Walt. Just fine."

"How are you, Mr. Riley?"

I nodded toward him, but didn't say anything.

"I found Mrs. Lewis's car," he said.

"Where?" Lewis and I asked simultaneously.

"Near St. Andrews," he said. "Right off Eleventh Street. There's a hospital or something nearby. We thought she might be there, but we searched it and she's not."

I stood. "I'll go see what I can find out about it."

Lewis stood with me and followed me to the door.

"I'm gonna find her," I said. "I did it before and I'll do it again."

"Before?" Lewis asked.

"Yeah," I said.

He looked as if he had no idea what I was talking about.

I glanced over at Walt. He had a wide-eyed look of concern on his face, but then he smiled and gave me an exaggerated wink.

"Right," I said. "Well, good night."

"I don't understand," Lewis was saying as I walked out.

"I'll explain everything to you, Mr. Lewis," Walt said.

I got in my car, cranked it up, drove off, and parked around the corner.

I could tell by his reaction, Lewis had never hired me to find his wife. Walt had. Was he working for Rainer? Had he killed Freddy, Margie, Cab, and July? When he left Lewises' a few minutes later, I followed him to try to find out.

Chapter 45

Walt led me right to the person he was working for, but it wasn't Rainer.

He drove across town to another large home, this one on the water near the Hathaway Bridge—which, just a few months back, had been closed for several days because a barge had crashed into its turntable. The timing had been bad, too. During the commissioning of the navy base, those involved had to cross the bay by boat.

The Spanish Colonial Revival house was white stucco with a red tile roof. Several of its windows were made of decorative turned wood and had balconies with wrought-iron railings. When the enormous, heavy carved wooden door of the house opened, Frank Howell, Harry's opposition for mayor, was standing on the other side.

After Howell closed the door, I made sure both my weapons were still secure, jumped out of the car, and ran toward the house.

Like Walt, I rang the doorbell. I then stood to the side and waited.

When Howell opened the door again, I pressed the barrel of my revolver into his forehead. Lifting his hands, he backed into the house very slowly. I followed. Even backing up under duress, Howell still shuffled his feet lightly like a dancer.

Walt whipped a pistol out of a shoulder holster beneath his coat and pointed it at me.

"Drop it," I said. "Or there'll be another candidate dropping out of the race—this one permanently."

He dropped his gun.

"Now kick it over to me."

He did.

"Now your other one."

He reached down into an ankle holster and withdrew a small .38 or .22.

"Careful," I said.

He dropped it on the floor, too, and kicked it over toward me.

Except for the room we were in, the house was dark. I knew Howell was a bachelor, but that didn't mean he didn't have guests or a staff.

"Who else is here?"

"It's just us," Howell said. "I swear."

"Get over there with him," I said, pushing the elephantine man toward his gunsel.

While watching Walt closely, I knelt down, laid my gun on the floor and quickly picked up his guns, pocketed them, then grabbed mine again. I figured he might make a run at me while I was awkwardly attempting to do with one hand what I needed two for, but he didn't.

"Where is she?" I asked.

"Who?" Howell asked, his voice filled with what seemed to be genuine surprise.

I shot Walt in the leg.

He let out a yelp and fell to the ground, clutching at the wound.

"In case either of you doubted the earnestness of my intentions," I said.

Blood was oozing out of the hole in Walt's trouser leg, and he writhed around in obvious pain, whimpering.

"Please," Howell said. "There's no need for—"

"Fuck, man," Walt was saying. "You fuckin'. . . I'm gonna fuckin' kill you. You hear me?"

"Where is Lauren?" I said.

"But y'all have her, surely," Howell said. "We do not."

I looked at Walt. He nodded vigorously. "I swear it."

"Did you kill Freddy and Margie?" I asked.

He didn't say anything, just continued to squirm and squeal.

I pointed the gun at him again and thumbed back the trigger.

"Answer him," Howell said. "Jesus. God. Just answer him."

"I was just looking for Mrs. Lewis's medical records," Walt said. His breathing was erratic and forceful, his voice cracking from the pain. "All they had to do was give them up. The tramp went through a hell of a lot for nothing. They were easy to find. Right under one of the cushions of her davenport."

"You followed me to her house," I said.

He nodded.

"Why kill Cab?" I asked. "Wasn't he working for you?"

"I didn't kill him," he said. "I thought the nigger did."

"Why'd you have to kill July?" I asked.

"Your secretary?" he said. "I had nothing to do with that. I swear."

I looked over at Howell.

He nodded. "He's telling the truth."

I thought about that for a moment—but just a moment, then I felt the barrel of a gun pressing against the base of my skull, and then it was all I could think about.

"Please be so kind as to drop your weapon and raise your hand above your head," a soft, high male voice with an accent said. It was Rainer.

I didn't move.

"I will shoot you, sir," he said. "I'd prefer not to, but believe me when I tell you I will."

"He will," Ann Everett said, as she stepped around from behind me.

Her blonde hair was still flipped out at the bottom, but she wasn't wearing her glasses. They had probably been a prop for the part she had been playing. Without her glasses, her green eyes appeared even smaller—or maybe it was the hardness in them.

"Don't look at me like that," she said. "None of this is personal. It's just politics. I don't like it any more than you do, but we all gotta swim in the same pond."

"You mean cesspool," I said.

"You're one to talk," she said. "Don't forget who started all this."

"Sir, I really must insist you drop your gun."

I did.

"And raise your hand."

I did.

Rainer stepped out from behind me as Ann picked up my gun. His dark eyes were flat, seemingly lifeless, his face dull and expressionless. His dark, wavy hair was more wiry than before and stood higher off his head.

Howell stood up. "Walt, can you walk?"

"Yeah, boss," he said. "I think I can."

"Then get these people out of here," he said.

"Whatta you want me to do with—"

"I don't care," he said. "I just don't want to be involved and I don't want to know."

"How are you going to force Lewis out of the campaign without any evidence?"

"We have evidence," Ann said. "We're not—"

"You talkin' about Lauren's medical records that were hidden in the clock?"

Her eyes widened.

"What's he talking about, Ann?" Howell asked.

"I don't know," she said.

"Were they hidden in a clock?"

She nodded, still staring at me.

"In the house on Cherry," I said. "Yeah."

"He's got them," she said.

"Do I?" I asked. "Or do the cops?"

"Where are they?" Rainer asked.

"I'll take you to them," I said.

Walt laughed. "That's rich. You'll take us to them." He looked at Howell. "I say we shoot him now and take our chances."

"Fine," he said. "Just don't do it here."

"I've already talked to Harry," I said. "He's not dropping out. He's got the—"

I kicked Ann into Rainer and ran out of the room, one of them firing a shot at me that missed and shattered a floor lamp next to the archway.

Ducking into the foyer, I pulled out one of Walt's guns and fired a round back into the room. I wasn't trying to hit anyone, just discouraging them from following me—which must have worked because they didn't.

"Give me the goddamn gun," Walt yelled.

"Here. Take it," Ann said.

"You gonna limp in here and shoot me?" I yelled.

I then fired two rounds into the room where they were and ran out the front door.

As I ran toward my car, I fired a few more rounds at the front door of Howell's mansion. With Walt wounded, I wasn't sure anyone would come after me. It'd be hard to imagine Everett, Howell, or Rainer chasing after me.

Once in my car, I sped away. After a mile or so, when I was certain they weren't following, I stopped at a payphone under a streetlamp in front of a closed service station and called Pete.

I told him all I could—all he needed to know to capture Rainer and the rest and to protect Harry. Next I called Harry and told him not to drop out of the race, Howell would. Then I hung up, got back in my car, and went to get Lauren.

Chapter 46

My headlights couldn't penetrate the fog. I was driving blind down Highway 22 towards Wewahitchka, to a fish camp on the Dead Lakes. Heat lightening continued to flicker occasionally, but there was no thunder in it. Mine was the only car on the highway, its engine the only sound.

Everything had fallen into place once I found out that Walt hadn't killed Cab or July, that Lauren's car was near Rainer's sanatorium, and Howell thought I knew where she was. Ray had her.

He was doing what he does—protecting, obsessing—this was Dorothy Powell all over again. My guess was he was as obsessed with her as I was, that he had been hired to follow her and had not stopped when the job ended. That's what July discovered in our logs—and why he killed her.

Ray had a small clapboard fish camp on the Dead Lakes and I was betting Lauren's life that he had taken her there.

When I pulled up in front of his camp and got out of my car, Ray walked out onto the porch holding his gun.

"Ray," I said.

"Jimmy," he said.

We were quiet a moment, the nocturnal noises of the woods the only sounds, the chirping of the crickets nearly deafening, maddening in its monotony.

"What're you doing?" I asked.

"Protecting her," he said.

"From?"

"Guys like you," he said.

"And Cab?"

He nodded, but didn't say anything.

Walt hadn't lied. He had no reason to. Ray had killed Cab. He had been following Lauren, attempting to protect her. It was how he knew Pete and Butch had taken me to look at Cab's crime scene—not from a friend at police headquarters.

I had been as wrong about Ray as I had about Lauren. My own distorted perceptions leading me to make the mistaken assumptions that always kept me a step behind. He hadn't been spending nearly as much time in court as he claimed. He had been following Lauren.

"But it was yourself you were protecting from July," I said.

His knees seemed to buckle a bit at that, and he had to steady himself against the railing, but he didn't say anything.

Beyond the cabin, the deadhead cypress trees rising out of the moonlit lake were eerie, their jagged edges traced in fog.

I looked at the cabin door. "Did you fall in love with Lauren when you were following her for Harry?" I asked.

"It's not like that," he said. "I just want to protect her."

"You're obsessed with her—or protecting her. You didn't stop following her when the job was over, did you?"

"I stopped," he said. "For a while."

"Not long I bet. And lately you've been back on but good, haven't you? Damsel in distress. Ray Parker's specialty. She thought

I was following her, but it was you. You were outside my hotel the night Lauren came to my room, but Freddy was, too, and I chased him. You're an elusive bastard, I'll give you that. I never got close enough to actually see you. But July did. She saw you that night in the park. It's why she was acting the way she was, why she went back to the office. She was looking at our logs for what I thought was the way I had covered up following Lauren when we first broke up, but it was actually your cover-up that she was confirming."

"I didn't mean to kill her," he said.

"I never thought you did," I said.

"I followed her back from the park."

"While I drove Lauren home and Clip took care of Carl—who you hired to distract us."

"I was just going to talk to her, but the way she looked at me . . ." He trailed off and was silent a long moment. "Like one of the goddamn perverts I put away. Like that Somerset fella. Just like that. I just couldn't take it. I . . . I lost it. She didn't understand. She couldn't."

"And if she told, you would lose your reputation," I said, "your agency."

He nodded.

"I was just trying to reason with her," he said, "but I was so angry, so . . . I slung her around a little . . . I thought I could calm her down, get her to see, but . . . she hit her head."

We were silent a long moment.

The dense woods around us made it seem like we were the only two people on the planet, the isolation nearly as palpable as my desperation.

"I'm here to get Lauren," I said. "She needs medical attention, and I'm taking her to get it."

"I'm gonna get a doctor out here in the morning," he said.

"Be too late. Besides, she's leaving with me tonight."

I took a couple of steps toward him and he pointed his gun directly at me.

"You gonna shoot me?" I asked.

"If I have to," he said.

"Ray, she's got to get help tonight. Might already be too late."

"Then I'll get her some help tonight," he said.

"She loves me," I said.

"Some women are only attracted to the wrong men for them."

"You talking about Dorothy or Lauren?"

He didn't say anything.

I took a few more steps toward him.

"I've got the drop on you," he said. "Could kill you easy even if I didn't."

"Do you hear yourself?" I said. "Kill me? Really? Ray?"

He didn't say anything, but I could see in his face he was willing to kill me.

I pulled out one of Walt's guns and pointed it at him as I continued to walk toward the house.

"Jimmy, don't make me shoot you," he said. "I don't want to. I truly don't."

My friend had become my enemy, my mentor my nemesis. I could tell he was willing to shoot me, but would he? Would he actually pull the trigger? Look me in the eye, kill me in cold blood?

"You're gonna have to," I said. "I'm here to get Lauren. She loves me. I love her. I owe her. She's leaving with me."

I continued walking toward him, going all in, betting my life he wouldn't shoot, feeling good about my chances right up until the moment he pulled the trigger.

The shot rang out through the woods, the rapport ricocheting off the pine, oak, and cypress trees, silencing all sounds.

I fell to the ground, searing pain in the right side of my abdomen. The acute ache of the wound was so intense I thought it unbearable, but then it vanished as quickly as it came, and I didn't feel anything at all.

The gun I was holding had fallen a few feet away. Ray stepped down off the porch and kicked it away from me.

"Toss your backup away and I won't shoot you again," he said.

I slowly reached down and pulled out the piece from my ankle holster and tossed it a few feet away.

"Smart boy," he said. "You're shot bad, but you might make it. You need to get to a doctor right away."

He reached down and started lifting me up. "Come on," he said. "I'll help you to your car."

As he lifted me, I came up with Walt's other gun and shot him straight in the heart at point-blank range. He let go of me and fell down. I fell on top of him.

It took me a few minutes, but I finally got up. My shirt was soaked with blood, and, as I climbed the steps to the cabin, I wondered how long I had before I lost consciousness and bled out.

Chapter 47

I stumbled into the cabin to find Lauren sleeping on the bed, relief washing over me to hear her breathing. I knelt down beside her and just watched her for a while.

Her beauty was heightened by her vulnerability as she laid there, her dark hair splayed out on the shoulders of her elegant white silk gown. She looked like the angel she had become.

She opened her eyes.

"Hey, soldier," she said.

"Hey."

As if to make sure I was real, she reached up and tenderly touched my face with the back of her delicate hand, and I imagined how abrasive my whiskers must be on her soft skin.

"I found you," I said.

"Thank God," she said.

"I'm so sorry," I said, fighting against the sting in the back of my eyes. "I . . ."

"I love you," she said.

For a long moment I couldn't speak. She had just said what I most wanted to hear and I didn't want to just move past it. I wanted to enjoy it, revel in it.

"I'm sorry for the all the cruel things I said to you."

"I forgave you the moment you did," she said. "You were speaking with the voice of love."

"It'd take someone like you to recognize it."

She smiled up at me. "How much do you know?"

"Everything."

"I'm glad."

"I've got to take you to a hospital," I said.

She shook her head. "I can't," she said. "I can't do that to Harry."

"Harry's fine," I said. "He'll be the next mayor of Panama City."

"Still, I can't—"

"Lauren, I'm taking you to a hospital."

"It's too late for the treatment now."

"You don't know that."

"I do," she said. "Just sit here with me for a while. You look tired."

I was tired. I was so tired. If I stopped, if I rested just for a moment, I'd never get up again.

"We have to go," I said. "Come on. I need you to help me."

"Okay, soldier," she said. "I'll go with you. I'll go with you anywhere. Just one condition. Take me somewhere other than Panama City and have me admitted as Lauren Riley."

Chapter 48

My jacket closed to keep the blood off her, Lauren was leaning on me as we drove toward Tallahassee in the diminishing fog.

Since losing my arm, I had not missed it as much as I did at this moment. I wanted to wrap it around her, to pull her close to me, to hold her tight.

I leaned down and kissed the top of her head. "I'm so sorry," I whispered. "I can't believe what I've done to you."

She looked up at me. "This isn't something you did to me. It's just something that happened. Too many things went into it for you to be the blame. We're both guilty."

I shook my head. "I'm—"

Covering my lips with her fingertips, she said, "You're my epiphany, my very own love letter from God. He used you to change my life, Jimmy."

"I—"

"Don't rush past that, soldier," she said. "Listen to me. In the whole universe, you were the one thing that could convince me of God's love. I'm dying. And I wouldn't change a thing—not a single moment—except to spend more of them with you. I'm thankful, not resentful."

I leaned in and kissed her forehead.

"I'm just glad you found me," she said. "I was so afraid I'd die alone."

"You're not gonna die," I said.

"Come on, soldier," she said. "We both are. You gotta face—"

"If I can be an epiphany and you can be a saint . . . anything's possible."

"Well," she said, "see what you can do, soldier."

I did.

I drove as fast as I could, speeding past deer grazing on the shoulder of the road, atop the moon-dappled pine-tree patterns on the grass, my old Ford piercing the remaining wisps of fog.

She fell asleep again, her breathing loud and labored.

I drove out of Gulf County and into Calhoun, over the Apalachicola River at Scott's Ferry, through Blountstown, over the Apalachicola River again, and into Bristol—the serpentine river coiling around us, slithering in the moonlight.

I felt lightheaded, as if I might pass out, but I kept driving.

I raced down Highway 20, through Hosford and past the turnoff to Wakulla Springs.

I wouldn't stop, no matter what.

The gas gauge needle was bouncing on E, but I kept driving.

I felt as if I had nearly bled out, as if everything around me were spinning, as if I didn't have the strength to even turn the wheel, but I kept driving.

I could no longer hear Lauren breathing beside me, no matter how hard I listened, but I kept driving. And I wouldn't stop. No matter what. I wouldn't accept any fate but the one I wanted, the one she deserved.

Just outside Tallahassee, I regained consciousness when I ran off the road and sideswiped a light pole. We were close, and I was still alive. Beside me, I thought I heard Lauren breathing, but I couldn't be sure, and I was afraid to check.

Directly in front of us, the rising sun burnished the buildings of Florida's capital and emblazoned the tops of pine trees along the eastern horizon. I was witnessing the birth of a new day, and it gave me hope. Maybe I had been right after all. Maybe anything was possible. Maybe we really could get through this. We had survived the night, hadn't we?

Acknowledgements

For support and encouragement and invaluable contributions:

Adam Ake, Jennifer Jones, Linda Macbeth, Marlene Womack, Lynn Wallace, Jill Mueller, Bette Powell, Fran Oppenheimer, Amy Moore-Benson, Jason Hedden, Emily Balazs, Ben Leroy, Graham Greene, Michael Connelly, Raymond Chandler, James Lee Burke, Dave Murray, Robert B. Parker, Mike and Judi Lister, Aimee Walsh, Jan Waddy, Dave Lloyd, Todd Sparks, Terry Lewis, Jack Saunders, Lou Boxer, Tony Simmons, River Jordan, Ansley Henkel, Jeff Moore, Jennifer Bonaventura, Rich Henshaw, Jon Jordan, Jen Forbus, Alison Janssen, Rod Wiethop, Pam and Micah and Meleah Lister, Travis Roberson, and Harley Walsh.

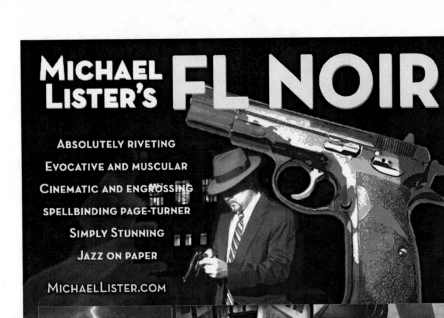

The Sussex Bay Foundation

Put Your Money Where Your Art Is!

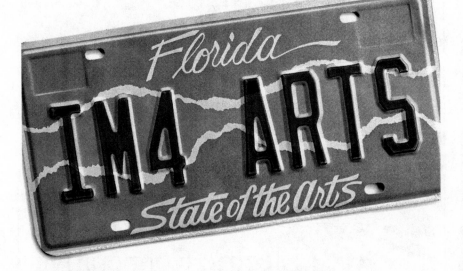

$20 from the sale of each arts tag goes to support the arts in your county!

BAY ARTS ALLIANCE

Bay County, Florida's Local Arts Agency

BayArts.org

TODD SPARKS IS
BOOKED EXCLUSIVELY THROUGH
GTS ENTERTAINMENT GROUP, INC.

MY COMPANY,GTS ENTERTAINMENT GROUP,
HAS BEEN MAKING EVENTS
GREAT FOR OVER 25 YEARS.

WE SPECILAIZE IN PREMIER ENTERTAINMENT
FOR ANY GATHERING AS WELL AS OFFER AN ARRAY OF
SERVICES BASED UPON YOUR TASTE, NEEDS AND
BUDGET. GTS ENTERTAINMENT CAN SAVE YOU TIME,
MONEY, AND ENHANCE THE QUALITY OF YOUR
SPECIAL OCCASION!

GTS ENTERTAINMENT GROUP, INC.
A FULL SERVICE ENTERTAINMENT AND EVENT AGENCY
FL. LIC. – TA-625

850.747.0903 or 1.888.683.1962
WWW.GULFTALENTSERVICES.COM

Michael Lister

A native Floridian, award-winning novelist, Michael Lister grew up in North Florida near the Gulf of Mexico and the Apalachicola River where most of his books are set.

In the early 90s, Lister became the youngest chaplain within the Florida Department of Corrections—a unique experience that led to his critically acclaimed mystery series featuring prison chaplain John Jordan: POWER IN THE BLOOD, BLOOD OF THE LAMB, FLESH AND BLOOD, THE BODY AND THE BLOOD, and BLOOD SACRIFICE.

Michael won a Florida Book Award for his literary thriller, DOUBLE EXPOSURE, a book, according to the *Panama City News Herald*, that "is lyrical and literary, written in a sparse but evocative prose reminiscent of Cormac McCarthy." His other thrillers include THUNDER BEACH, BURNT OFFERINGS, and SEPARATION ANXIETY.

Michael also writes a popular weekly column on art and meaning and life titled *Of Font and Film* (www.OfFontandFilm.com), which includes reviews of film and fiction.

His website is www.MichaelLister.com.

CPSIA information can be obtained at www.ICGtesting.com
Printed in the USA
240003LV00002B/2/P